"Anytime you're ready, Johnson."

Willie readied his hand.

The stranger wet his lips in anticipation of the duel. Willie saw that the man enjoyed the killing, the excitement. Such a man would die sooner or later. And Willie had more to do with his life.

The cold determination, the anger that had brought him through a war, through Comanche raids and cattle drives came back to him. His eyes flashed that chilling anger across to Johnson, and the killer's smile fell away.

It was Johnson's hand that moved first, taking the twin revolvers from their holsters even as Willie drew his Colt....

The Trident Brand

G. CLIFTON WISLER

FAWCETT GOLD MEDAL • NEW YORK

A Fawcett Gold Medal Book
Published by Ballantine Books
Copyright © 1982 by G. Clifton Wisler

All rights reserved under International and Pan-American Copyright Conventions. Published in the United States by Ballantine Books, a division of Random House, Inc., New York, and simultaneously in Canada by Random House of Canada Limited, Toronto.

Library of Congress Catalog Card Number: 81-43153

ISBN 0-449-13020-7

This edition published by arrangement with Doubleday and Company, Inc.

All the characters in this book are fictitious, and any resemblance to actual persons, living or dead, is purely coincidental.

Manufactured in the United States of America

First Ballantine Books Edition: October 1986

This book is dedicated to my brother David.

CHAPTER 1

Ψ

It was early. The sun hung in the cloudless eastern sky like a huge orange globe. The bright glowing sphere seemed frozen, held in place by some invisible hand. Looking west, everything appeared cast in fresh bronze. Even the broad river took on a golden tint.

The river. It was the river which brought green to the land, which provided water for stock and crops, that washed the dust and the sweat from the weary shoulders of those men who scratched out their existence along its banks.

Giver of life, the Indians called it. Years afterward it had been given a new name by the pale-skinned settlers who'd carved farms out of the rugged country that lined its more southern waters. They'd named it Brazos.

Just another place name. Just another word for just another of the rivers which crossed the seemingly endless Texas plain. But for one, the word spelled the end of a long journey, a link to a past, a strange kind of belonging in the midst of a world which had become pointless, cruel, alien.

As the sun rose higher, a single man could be seen on a

1

barren hillside. Not quite six feet tall, slight of build, more the shape of a boy than a man. But as the figure took form, there was no mistaking the firm shoulders, the tanned and weathered skin of a warrior.

A bright flash of light reflected off the steel scabbard of a saber worn at the man's hip. The silvery light revealed a severe face. The stubble of a week's growth of beard covered cheeks that might otherwise have held the tint of youth. Dark blond hair hung in long unkempt strands beneath a tall gray hat.

Thin lines appeared on the man's forehead, reminders of difficult decisions and hard times. His chin was solid, firm, arrogant enough to command respect. But it was the eyes of the man that marked him most.

They were a grayish shade of blue, like the river. But there was nothing bright, nothing that hinted of life in those eyes. They were cold, remote. It was as if they could see what wasn't there. Something terrible and unspoken lurked within those eyes. There was pain, and hatred, and suffering, more than was imaginable in eyes that had seen but twenty years of life.

The eyes had been what had made him feared by his enemies. Whatever made those eyes hard and lifeless made the man fearless and unpredictable. Even death seemed to fear his awful glance. So it had seemed to those who had ridden with him.

It was this fearlessness that had made him noteworthy as a soldier. He could ride through the fires of perdition, the colonel had said once. He would gallop through volleys of musket fire that would sweep away a full company. But there he would be, waving that wicked saber, the pale blue flag with the single white star at his side.

The war had been over a year, though. The long lines of horsemen had thinned so that only handfuls had remained to stack their rifles in a meadow near an obscure Virginia courthouse. The memory of it brought fire to the man's eyes. He remembered the humiliating way the Yanks had cheered their defeated enemies. And he'd ridden west a beaten man, conquered.

His clothes showed it. They were little more than rags. Homespun cloth dyed butternut. Only his coat, once heavy wool, held its original shape. His trousers were threadbare, patched so many times the inside resembled one of his mother's quilts. He had a good pair of boots, taken from a dead Michigan lieutenant at Five Forks.

Five Forks. That was where the company'd made their final charge. It was where Nathan Chalmers had his head blown off his shoulders. It was where Keller and Thompson had been taken. Five Forks, where that devil of a Yank general had ridden across the Virginia countryside laughing and singing.

Rascal, the horse he'd inherited from the colonel, was killed that day, shot three times. The poor creature had carried the young man close to four miles, her life flowing out of her. And he'd almost been captured by a patrol of New Yorkers looking for firewood.

He'd gotton away, though. He patted the tall chestnut gelding beside him as he remembered taking it from a startled Ohio colonel. Spoils of war. He'd plastered the poor horse's rump with mud so the Yank guards couldn't see the U.S. branded there when the Army surrendered at Appomattox. And he'd ridden the horse all the way to Texas.

His eyes softened as he looked closely at the river. He thought he saw someone on the far side, a bare-chested boy of ten perhaps, running through the water with a young Indian friend. But it was only the shadows of the morning, only memories neglected too long.

Spring rains are late this year, he thought to himself. The farmers would have a poor crop. Growing corn in mesquite country was hard enough without drought. Much safer to be a cattleman along the Brazos.

He searched the lightening horizon for signs of cattle. He thought he heard the sounds of a herd on the wind, but

3

he saw nothing. No . . . there was something. There, just beyond that stand of juniper.

The anger returned to his eyes as he recognized what it was. Thin lines of wire held in place by crooked posts of mesquite and live oak. Fences. Fences had come to his beloved valley.

I hate fences, he said to himself. I hate the way they bring towns and roads and people. I hate the way they take away a man's freedom to ride the land like God intended it should be ridden, with the wind in your face and the sun on your naked shoulders. And the stars to light the way at night.

The fences were there, though, staking down the boundary of the ranch, marking the beginning of one place and the ending of another. On a small strip of leather nailed to one of the posts he noticed something. A brand. The thin black outline of a three-pronged fork.

A trident. It brought a stir to his chest. He remembered holding down calves as his father applied the branding iron to their rumps. That same trident brand, the mark of the Delamers.

It had been his father's idea. The man had read somewhere that the trident was the symbol of the sea god, Neptune. Delamer was the American version of the name chosen by the old one, the greatgrandfather who'd crossed the Atlantic on his way to New Orleans back in the last century. De la Mer. Of the sea. That was what it meant in French. When the family first came to Texas, they'd run all the letters together into one word.

Delamer. It was his name, too. William J. Delamer III. A right fancy name, the colonel had said. His father's name. His grandfather's name. A name to be proud of, a name of distinction.

"Never forget you're a Delamer, son," his father had said as they rode away from the same valley he was staring at that moment. "Remember the legacy. Delamers always stand in the first rank when there's fighting to be done. They stand tall. Others can follow. A Delamer leads."

4

His lip quivered as he remembered the other words his father had spoken, the words mumbled with dying breath on that rainy night following the bloody first day at Shiloh.

"Willie, be as hard as the land. Build the ranch. Prove your courage. Show them all you had what the old one had, the strength to go on when the rest gave up."

"I will, Papa," he'd said, his sixteen-year-old eyes growing hard and dark as his father passed off into the night.

The promise had been kept ever since then. It'd been kept the second day at Shiloh when the regiment had been thinned like a herd before slaughter. He'd kept it the deadly July afternoon when they'd charged across a Pennsylvania wheatfield and struggled in the scorching heat of the Devil's Den, only to fall back to Virginia when Pickett failed to break the Yank center.

It hadn't been easy. When the woods had caught fire in The Wilderness, he'd wanted to run from the hell of burning flesh and the screams of the wounded. In the cold and wet of the Petersburg line, even at Five Forks, he'd fought on, though giving up would have been simple.

The memories faded, and he looked again at the rugged countryside below him. On a distant hill stood a lone mesquite tree, bathed in the morning sunlight so that it stood stark and black against the horizon. He was like that tree, alone and defiant. All those long months of riding from Virginia he'd longed for the comfort of his mother's shoulder, the security of the home he'd known as a boy. As he stared at the tree, he wondered if that comfort would truly be waiting just another three miles away.

"Hey, Major!" someone shouted from the other side of the hill. "Got a spot of coffee and some eggs 'bout ready for fryin'."

Willie gently nudged the gelding into a trot. The horse threaded its way down the embankment, then entered the crude encampment at the base of the hill.

"You're up early, Willie," said another voice, this one belonging to his old friend Travis Cobb. "Hungry for home?"

"It's been a long time," Willie said, dismounting.

5

"Five years," Travis said.

"You been gone since '61, Major?" the man cooking the eggs asked. "How you come to do that?"

"His father commanded the Second Texas at Shiloh, Bates," Travis said. "Led the charge that pushed them Ohio boys out of the Wicker Field. Took a musket ball for his trouble. Died that very night."

"Sorry," the cook said, frowning. "Didn't know, Major."

"Nothing to be sorry over, Bates," Willie said. "Men get killed in battle."

"But not our major, eh, Slocum?" Bates said, nudging a fourth man awake.

"No, sir," Slocum said, accepting a cup of hot coffee.

Willie took a cup, too, and the fifth man in their party, a young man of seventeen named Bentley, finally rose.

"We part company today, boys," Travis said, taking a rag and giving his boots a brief wipe. "My sister Ellen's goin' to have to cook my breakfast."

The mention of Ellen's name stirred another memory in Willie's chest, but he fought it.

"She'll be wantin' you for supper tonight, Willie," Travis said. "And more than that 'fore long."

The other men hooted and hollered, but a hard stare from Willie silenced them.

"Not tonight, Trav," Willie finally said. "I've got my family to see. Tomorrow'd be better."

"Then tomorrow it is," Travis said. "Give my best to your ma."

"Will do that," Willie said, clasping his friend's hand firmly. It wasn't easy for either of them to let go. Since they'd ridden off together five years before, no day had passed when they were far from each other.

"Tomorrow, and that's a promise, right?" Travis asked.

"My word, sir," Willie said, giving a mock bow.

"You boys want to drop by for a sip of Pa's corn liquor?" Travis asked the others. "Guaranteed to put hair on your chest, Bentley."

The older men laughed at Bentley's red face.

6

"It'd be best for us to head on down the valley," Bates said, speaking for all of them. "Ain't seen my missus in three winters, nor my little ones, neither. Got the urge to feel 'em all around me just now."

Travis nodded.

"Guess this is good-bye for me, too, boys," Willie said. "My ranch is just over the hill there. You're welcome to visit if you'd like."

"Like Bates said, Major, we got the urge to see home again," Slocum said. "It's been our privilege to serve you, sir. If them Yanks take up the notion to go messin' with the Bonnie Blue flag again, you just look us up."

Willie swallowed the sadness he felt looking at the faces in front of him. There'd been a time when the company had numbered a hundred strong. Five out of a hundred wasn't much of a showing.

"Know what you're thinkin', Major," Bates said. "Guess we all wish a few more of the boys'd made it back."

"We left a lot of Yank widows, Major," Bentley said, laughing. "Heck, another hundred Brazos Raiders and we'd've kicked old Grant all the way to Boston."

"No," Willie said, a deep frown on his face. "You remember Five Forks, Tom Bentley. You remember Jimmy Bradley's face all blown apart back at the Trinity crossing. You go home and thank the Lord you're lucky it wasn't you."

"Major?" Bates said, his eyebrows wide with surprise.

"Just tellin' it how it is," Willie said. "I plan to put my saber away and do a little ranchin'. Wish you boys good fortune with your crops."

"Get them injun friends of yours to do a rain dance," Slocum said. "Won't be no summer corn 'less it rains some."

Willie sat down as Bates turned the eggs and spooned them onto four tin plates. Willie ate the blackened breakfast without complaining. He'd stopped tasting food when they'd started eating rats in the Petersburg trenches.

"Right fine eatin', them eggs," Bates said, shoveling a spoonful into his mouth.

"Yessiree," Bentley said, smiling.

Willie stood up then and looked them over. The three men came to a stiff attention and saluted.

"Gentlemen, it's been a hard couple of years," Willie said, returning the salute. "I've come to know and trust you. But now it's time I was ridin'."

"Good luck, sir," Bates said, shaking Willie's hand.

"And you the same, Bates."

Willie shook each man's hand in turn, then walked over to where his old pack mule was waiting. He'd already tied the heavy war chest on the beast's back. Now he led the creature over and tied its reins to his saddle horn.

"Adios, Raiders," Willie said, rearing his horse into the air and waving his hat. In another moment he was riding westward, a lone horseman silhouetted against the horizon.

CHAPTER 2

Ψ

Willie rode slowly across the broken ground. Deep gullies had been carved over the years by torrential rains, and gopher holes appeared from time to time. More than one fine horse had broken a leg in such country.

As he came to the first fence, he found himself smiling. It wasn't the fence itself. He could never feel anything but contempt for the long strands of wire and wooden posts. But he looked past the wire, past the gnarled junipers to the high cliffs across the river.

Castle Cliffs they were called. His father had told Willie they'd been named by the first Spaniards who'd explored the area. They stood towering above the river, far above the lower northern bank of the river.

Many times he'd climbed those cliffs. There was an ancient Indian village there, or what was left of one anyway. It was the home of the ancient ones, the natives who'd roamed the valley before time and the Comanches had killed the last of them.

Their burial ground remained, an eerie acre filled with

9

rotting scaffolds and bleached bones, old war trophies and decaying blankets. Strange sounds could be heard there at night. The Comanches believed it to be a place of powerful medicine.

Willie had gone there to pray. The first time he was but eight years old. His brother Stephen was down with a fever, and he'd wanted to do something to help. Old Yellow Shirt, the Comanche chief, had often told stories of how medicine chiefs bled themselves to gain favor with the spirits. Willie had cut his wrists so that bright red blood flowed over his hands. He'd felt a strange presence on the cliffs, but when he'd returned home, Stephen was dead.

Two years later when his father announced Willie could go on the annual deer hunt, the boy'd climbed the cliff to pray for strength and courage. At his side had been Red Wolf, Yellow Shirt's only living son. The two boys had prayed side by side, each in his own way. Then they'd gone out and shot deer, two fine bucks each.

Willie had gone other times as well, before leaving home that terrible summer before the war. His father wanted him to go to the fine gentlemen's school in New Orleans that Willie's brother, Sam, had attended. The thought of leaving the beloved valley was more than Willie could stand. For months he'd lived with the Comanches, hunting buffalo and riding the plains.

The last time he'd gone to the cliff had been the night before leaving the valley at his father's side. It was the one thing he'd never been able to explain to his mother, that need to stand on the cliff and speak with whatever was there. It was impossible to share the sense of inner peace that had come to him there. It was part of the magic that tied him to the land, to the cliffs and the river and the rocks.

Willie's cold eyes swept across the cliff, searching for the old lances that marked the burial place of some great chief of the ancient ones. He'd always been able to see them but his eyes were not so keen as before, though. He couldn't find the spot. Perhaps the wind or the rains had finally swept away the old lances.

He turned away from the cliffs and nudged his horse into motion. It felt good riding that morning. It was a strange thing, Willie and horses. Out of the saddle he'd always found himself wanting. He'd never been big. When he'd fought Red Wolf in mock combat, the Indian had given him a lance thrust which had left a jagged scar on his left arm. Later only the quickness of his hands and his cleverness had kept him alive those years in the Shenandoah Valley, at Gettysburg and The Wilderness. The same ability to think on horseback kept him out of a Union stockade after Five Forks.

He pulled his horse to a stop then, and it whined nervously.

"What is it, Thunder?" Willie asked.

The horse shuddered, and Willie listened. He could hear cattle moaning to the west. Delamer cattle. My cattle, he thought.

"It's all right, boy," Willie told the horse. "No Yanks to fight this morning."

The horse seemed to understand. It picked up its pace, so much so that Willie had to shorten his reins in order to keep pace with the slow mule behind him.

"Eager to show your speed, huh?" Willie asked.

He'd named the horse Thunder since that first night when it'd run half the day past cannons and Yank patrols, never even breathing hard. Run like thunder, he remembered his father telling him; when you're in a fix, run like thunder.

It had become ride like thunder, strike like lightning, hit hard, fall back, hit again. Those were the colonel's tactics. Willie doubted they'd be much use on a cattle ranch. It would undoubtably have been better if he'd gone to New Orleans and learned whatever it was a gentleman rancher needed to know.

Up ahead the trees parted, and a small road appeared. There was a gate in the fence, and Willie opened it. He led his two animals through, then closed and fastened the gate. Moments later he was riding through familiar ground, the

11

east pasture. In it were hundreds of cattle, more stock than Willie could have imagined.

"Old General Lee'd won the war with a herd like this," he said, smiling at the animals. "If we'd had enough to eat, I believe we'd have marched straight to Washington City instead of to Appomattox."

Willie waved to two ranch hands ahead. Both were new men, boys really. The war had taken a toll of the men in the valley. He figured any boy twelve or older was likely doing a man's job.

The hands gave him hard stares. They hadn't seen many cavalry majors riding through their herd. But the cattle were restless that morning, and the hands attended to their work and left the stranger to his business.

Willie rode on, passing the old cabin Mitch Simms had put up back in '44. Simms was one of his father's first hands, an independent type. Old Mitch preferred the cabin to the barn where the other hired men slept. Willie'd stayed over a couple of times in the cabin. It smelled of damp leather. To Willie the barn was a big improvement.

The road he'd been following dwindled to a narrow path, but Willie followed it onward. He knew where the house was. It sat on a hill overlooking the whole of the river. The ranch straddled two great bends of the Brazos, either of which would have been enough land for three families. But it was the dream of Big Bill Delamer to build a ranch that would stretch from one bend to the other and include all the land drained by each bank of the river.

Willie's heart began pounding as he climbed the hill at last. The old white house made of oak planks and native stone was just ahead. Home at last. His mother's soft shoulder and his sister's rolling laughter. Those brown eyes of his brother James growing wider as he told some old Indian legend Red wolf or Yellow Shirt had passed along to him.

As Thunder topped the crest of the hill, Willie's heart died. The hardness returned to his eyes. The old house, the place he remembered with such affection, was gone. Only

12

the charred remains of scorched timbers and a few discarded kitchen utensils were left.

The two tall barns which had flanked the house had vanished, too. Willie wondered what could have happened. He could see how one of the buildings might burn, but all three? It couldn't have been an accident.

And what of his family? Had they perished with the house? He suddenly grew anxious. A wide road led from the river past the house and on northward. Willie urged Thunder toward that road, then pulled the mule along.

Willie's anxiety was partly soothed by a second great herd of cattle. This herd was grazing close to the river on a section of land where the Comanches once made their campus. Good grass grew there, and two small springs fed a creek which split the pasture.

His worrying was reduced further by tracks made in the sandy road by a small carriage. His mother traveled in such a vehicle.

Another three or four miles were crossed before his curiosity was satisfied, though. At the base of a broad mesa, close to where the river made its second great bend, stood an enormous white structure the likes of which Willie hadn't seen since leaving Shreveport months before.

"My God," he said out loud. "What is this?"

He rode along, stopping when he entered a grand courtyard. The fine house stood in the center of a clearing, a full two stories high, with red shingles on the roof and one of those weather vanes like they had on all the big houses back in Virginia. Six tall wooden columns lined a great veranda in front of the house. The porch appeared appeared to be made of native stone.

It was a great house. To the right stood a stable and a smokehouse. To the left were two small outbuildings, probably quarters for servants or such. Willie shook his head to make sure he wasn't seeing things. It was like visiting one of the huge plantations which lined the Mississippi River.

He rode to the stable, halting as a tall young man strode out to meet him.

"Sir, may I help you?" the stable hand asked.

"Could be," Willie said. "This the Delamer house?"

"This is Mr. Delamer's home, headquarters of the Trident Ranch."

"The Trident Ranch?" Willie asked, surprised it was no longer enough to call the place by his father's name as before. "Well, I'd like to see Mrs. Delamer."

The youth stared at Willie. Apparently gentlemen callers were expected to be more presentable. Willie might have volunteered to wash some of the dust off if he hadn't come two thousand miles in twelve months just to see his family again. He slid off the horse and handed the reins to the stable boy. Then he started for the house.

"Sir?" the stable hand asked. "You can't just walk up there like you own the place."

Willie turned to the young man and laughed.

"Don't you see, I do. See my horse is fed and watered. I've ridden a long way, and I won't have need of him more today. Tend my mule, too. You can set the trunk out. I'll come fetch it myself."

Willie walked across the open ground, whistling to himself. Lush gardens bordered the stone walks which led to the house. Willie marveled at it. Flowers had a difficult time in the Texas heat. Someone had given the garden a lot of care.

He was met at the door by a large black man. His presence surprised Willie more than the house. There'd never been any Negroes on the ranch before the war. Bill Delamer was opposed to slavery, and what Big Bill opposed you saw little of in the valley.

"Take your hat, sir?" the black man asked.

"Who are you?" Willie asked, handing over his hat.

"Matthew," the man said. "You been to the war, sir?"

"Some," Willie said. "Is Mrs. Delamer in?"

"She here," the man said. "You got a name?"

"Tell her it's her son," Willie said, laughing.

"Yes, sir," the man said, giving Willie a strange look as he walked on down the hall.

14

The man's departure gave Willie a chance to examine the inside of the house. A great stairway led to the second floor. To one side of the foyer was a parlor, complete with piano. On the other side was a small sitting room. Beautiful carpets covered the floors, and paintings of New Orleans river scenes and Mississippi steamboats adorned the walls.

Willie then heard small feet on the floor. He turned and watched the approach of a lovely lady in her late twenties, dressed in a fine yellow gown. Matthew followed her at a respectful distance.

"Sir, you have us at a disadvantage," the lady said.

Willie frowned. He'd been expecting his mother.

"Sir, is something wrong?" the woman asked.

"I'm sorry," he said. "I was looking for my mother."

"Matthew said something to that effect," she told him.

The words began rolling around inside Willie's head. A trace of recognition came at last. This had to be Helen, his brother Sam's wife. Strange that five years could so change a person.

"Helen?" he asked.

"I beg your pardon," the woman said, alarmed.

"You want I should fetch Mr. James?" Matthew asked.

"I'm sorry I startled you, Helen," Willie said. "I hardly recognized you, not to mention my surprise at this house. When I left, you were all still living down by the river."

"When you left?" she asked.

"Yes," he told her. "I'm Willie, Willie Delamer."

"Dear God," she said, grasping the arm of a chair to keep from fainting. "We all thought you were dead."

"As you can see, I'm not," Willie said, forcing a smile to his face. "I trust you'll excuse me, Helen, but I'm eager to see everyone else. Where's Mama?"

"Five years is a long time, Willie," she said, motioning for Matthew to leave. "You'll find many things changed."

"Where's Mama?" Willie asked again, his eyes growing hard and cold as he felt a new urgency to see his mother.

"If you've been down to the old house, you must have

15

passed her, Willie. She's on the little knoll just past Juniper Spring."

"What?" he asked, remembering the place. "That's where we buried Stephen."

"Yes, it is," she said softly.

"I don't understand," he said, stammering. "Mama's dead? How?"

"We had some hard times here, Willie."

"I can see that," he said, staring at the finery in the front rooms of the house.

"There was a bad dry spell the summer of '62. Your mama was grieving for Papa. We had an outbreak of the cholera. It spread along the river like wildfire. Mama took it on herself to help tend the sick. When she got it herself, she refused to rest. It was too much for her."

"I should have been here," he said, grinding his teeth to conceal the anger inside him.

"It might have been different if you had, but I doubt it. Your mama was close to forty years old. Most of those years were spent in this godforsaken wilderness. I think she just wore herself out."

"Mama? No, she loved life. Even when Christine and Stephen died, she wouldn't cry over them. She told James and me we just had to be better because they wouldn't be around to help build the ranch."

"She changed after Papa rode off to war, Willie. Sam and I thought she might go to Jacksboro and live with Mary. But her roots were here. She was good with the children, but I don't think they made her laugh like Papa could."

"No, Papa was the best."

"I'm sorry to have been the one to spoil your homecoming, Willie. If Sam were around, I'd have sent for him. He's ever so much better at saying things than I am."

"You did it most . . . most . . . delicately, Helen. I thank you."

"You're most kind."

"Where is Sam?" Willie asked.

"At the county seat. You likely don't know about all the

trouble the Yankee garrisons at the forts are causing. They won't keep the Indians away, but they're forever bringing us some new tax or another. Why, we've paid more taxes this last year than in all the time your father held this land."

"A lot of people back East are having to sell their homes," Willie told her. "Sheridan burned half the Shenandoah Valley. Down in Mississippi the carpetbaggers are turning over whole plantations to the Negroes. Turning widows and small children out in the streets."

"That's simply horrid," Helen said. "We've heard such nightmare talk."

"Fortunately I see we've got cattle. There's more than enough market for beef up North."

"But no way to get them there," she said, sighing. "Our herds grow larger, but there's no railhead within several hundred miles. Most of the South's rolling stock was destroyed or confiscated during the war. The Yankees won't help. They're determined to force us into ruin."

Willie sat down a minute and listened to her describe the new laws and taxes the federally appointed judges and governors had established. It all spelled trouble for the Trident Ranch or Delamer Ranch or whatever it was now called.

"I'll do anything I can to help," Willie said, trying to fight the frown off his face.

"An extra hand we won't have to pay is always a help," she said.

Willie frowned. He started to say something, then stopped. He'd always figured the ranch was his to run. It was as much as promised by his father. He'd just learned of his mother's death, though, and Helen wasn't the one to discuss the estate of his father with. That would be for Sam and James and Willie to decide with Judge Taylor in Palo Pinto.

Willie's thoughts were interrupted by the sound of hooves on the road outside. Matthew announced the arrival of Mr. James Delamer, and Willie flew out the door to greet his brother.

17

CHAPTER 3

Ψ

The tall young man dismounted from his horse with a grace befitting a gentleman of wealth and position. For a minute Willie thought he was back in Richmond. A stable boy took the horse and led it away. Then the young gentleman walked toward the house.

Willie studied the figure. He was tall for fourteen. Dark black hair fell across a tanned forehead, and deep hazel eyes flashed out a certain sense of command, poise. Presence they would have called it back East. The youth walked with a long stride that could almost have been called a swagger.

Willie wanted to rush out and embrace this brother he'd not seen in five long years, but something held him back. Perhaps it was the sadness that was only now making itself felt over the news of his mother's death. It might have been the shock over the changes that had come to the ranch. But mostly he supposed it was the look of contempt that flashed across his younger brother's face when Willie was finally noticed.

"Excuse me, Major," James said, bowing slightly. "I've had a hard ride, and I'd like to wash before dining."

As the young man eased around Willie's shoulder, Helen stopped him.

"James, you haven't been introduced to our guest," she said, smiling so that the boy's face lost a great deal of its hostility.

"Oh, I beg your pardon," James said. "I didn't realize you were a guest. You must understand that we have a great many veterans riding through in search of work."

"I can imagine," Willie said, his eyes growing colder. "I expect to be here quite some time, however."

James's face became white as the words were spoken. The boy's eyes warmed, and his hands began to tremble.

"Willie?" the young man said, gasping.

"So you recognize me at last, do you?" Willie said, his heart warming some.

"But . . . how? We heard you were killed."

"No, my hide's just too tough for any old minie ball to scratch," the cavalryman said, trying to manage a bit of laughter. "You've grown."

"Into a man," Helen said, interrupting. "But surely this reunion can await. You both look in need of some refreshment."

"And a trip to the river," Willie said, glancing at his dusty clothes.

"We don't go to the river anymore," James said. "We have a fine steel tub you bathe in right in your own bedroom. Matthew, see to it water is heated," the young man commanded, nodding to the servant.

"I have a trunk in the stable," Willie said, starting down the steps.

"I'll see to it, sir," Matthew said as James caught Willie's arm.

"We have servants to tend to such things," the younger brother said. "Now, Helen, where shall we put our returning hero?"

"I wasn't prepared for company," she said. "Perhaps the children might surrender one of their rooms."

"What of the guest room?" James asked.

"Sam is expecting a visit from . . . from a gentleman in the government," she said.

"Oh," James said, his face growing pale. "Well, there's certainly space enough for two in my room. Come along, big brother. It looks as if we're once again roommates."

Willie caught a sparkle in James's eyes, and it brightened up the moment. He followed his brother up the fine stairway and down a hall to a room overlooking the open courtyard behind the house.

"We haven't done so poorly in your absence, have we?" James asked as they entered the room.

"When was all this built?" Willie asked.

"Sam started the house after the Comanches burned the old one a third time. He decided to put an end to the Indian trouble once and for all. They burned half the valley, you know. They carried away women and children, stole fifty head of cattle from us alone.

"Well, Sam led a company of militia and wiped out most of the troublemakers. What were left took off across the Red River. We still get raided from time to time, but they stay clear of the ranch proper."

"And this house?"

"Sam brought in an architect from New Orleans. Helen's cousin. Most of the timber was cut up on the Trinity and run through a sawmill. Wagon after wagon brought it in. The stone's all cut from the county."

"And the finery?" Willie asked. "You don't find rugs like these on the Trinity."

"Most of that came after the war. Sam went down to New Orleans and bought up all sorts of things, mainly off old plantations. Some of the things came from Helen's mother. Better to sell cheap to a fellow Southerner than have the things taken for taxes by the Yanks."

"But where'd the money come from?"

"Sam signed contracts for cattle delivery. He supplied

the Confederacy for three years. We took payment in Colorado gold. Then since the Yanks have been here, we've been selling to them as well. We've done right well."

Willie sat down in a chair and stared out the window. Two small boys screamed at each other in the courtyard. Willie recognized a bit of his brother Sam in each.

"Helen will likely quiet them soon," James said. "The taller of the two is Robert. You remember him. The other is little Sam. There's a baby as well, Catherine. So the Delamers have expanded in a number of ways."

"You've been to school," Willie said, examining his brother closely.

"To an academy in Houston. Mama died, you know."

"Yes, Helen told me," Willie said, biting down on his lip.

"There wasn't much of a place for me here after that. Helen had her own little ones to look after, and Sam was busy with the ranch. You were away to the war, dead for all we knew. So Sam sent me to Houston. I've read all sorts of books. Next year I hope to read for the law. Sam says we'll have need of a lawyer in the family."

"I suppose," Willie said.

"And what are your plans, Willie? I don't suppose the Yanks will be needing any cavalry officers in their army."

"Not from Texas, at least."

"Then what? Mary's gone to Colorado, you know."

"Colorado?"

"She left a letter for you with Sam. I don't quite know why she left. Sam says it was because her husband Tom was bound to be conscripted into the army, but I doubt that. There are lots of men around here who weren't called up. The valley's always sent its share and more to the regiments up East."

"Do you hear from her?"

"Sure as the sun comes up. They've got a fine little farm going. There are two boys. She writes to say she still thinks of us. But you can tell she's happy there."

"Are you?" Willie asked, his face turned serious.

"Of course," James said, laughing. "I sometimes miss the old days when we used to ride across the hills and run through the river naked. But just look at the ranch. We've got money and power. There isn't a man for two hundred miles who doesn't know who the Delamers are."

Willie watched his brother's eyes fill with fire. It reminded him of how he must have looked when the colonel had handed him the woolen coat with the lieutenant's insignia stitched on the cuffs.

"Well, I suppose you'll be wanting to clean up," James said. "The wash basin's here, by the window. Matthew will bring in the tub and hot water. There's linen in this chest. Just make yourself at home. I've got a bottle of lilac water on the large chest there."

Willie followed his brother's hand as it pointed out the various places. Then there was a knock on the door. Matthew and another man carried in a big steel tub and set it near the corner of the room. Two large black women carried in buckets of steaming water and poured it in the tub. Then Matthew returned with Willie's trunk.

"When you finish, come to dinner," James said, dipping a cloth in the hot water and washing his face. "I'll be waiting."

"I won't be long," Willie promised.

"Take as long as you like. It would seem four years in the army would earn a man a few moments of ease."

Willie managed a smile for his brother and a nod to the servants. Each returned the gesture in kind. As the last of them left the room, Willie closed the door and began slipping out of his clothes. He removed the heavy saber and large army colt first. Then he shed his heavy boots and glanced at his dust-laden shins. The stockings were hopelessly riddled with holes, and his toes protruded bare and black.

He unbuttoned his uniform coat, then peeled off his ragged trousers. A moment later he was shed of his dirty underclothes. At last he sank with relief into the bathtub.

Willie never imagined water could be so welcome. He

took a bar of lye soap and scrubbed until his skin was red and raw. The dirt and dust loosened, darkening the tub so that he had to stand in order to avoid being immersed in mud.

As he glanced in a large looking glass over one of the two beds in the room, Willie sighed. He saw with regret how the war had aged him. His chest and face were bronzed and leathery. He rubbed the long red scar on his belly caused by a Yank saber in the Chancellorsville campaign.

There were other scars, too. The large one made by the hurried surgeon in Corinth. The smaller ones made by the general's doctor after two musket balls had found Willie's back in The Wilderness. There were thinner saber scars on his thighs, the old lance wound on his arm, smaller scrapes and bruises brought about by five years of living under an open sky.

The image in the mirror seemed too small, too young to be him. The face, except for those foreboding eyes, seemed almost as youthful as James's. His hair, once cut, would lose its wildness. His wiry shoulders hadn't lost all their boyishness. Even the curly brown hairs that had started growing on his chest had yet to become thick and matted like his father's.

Willie walked to the war chest and took out his razor. He slipped on a pair of clean drawers, saved especially for his homecoming, and lathered up the shaving soap.

He trimmed the whiskers from his cheeks, watching the image of the outcast, the ruffian, grow more presentable with each stroke. He carefully shaved the small hairs from his neck and those under his lower lip. He left the scant moustache, frowning that it had not grown dark and heavy like Travis Cobb's. In disappointment he finally shaved it off, too.

He dressed slowly, trying in vain to find clothing which had escaped the scourge of war. He had the old blue trousers the Second Texas had been outfitted in back in Houston. The pants had been abandoned after an Alabama sharpshooter put a bullet through old Oscar Hannah's rump that first day at Shiloh.

He wore the heavy gray tunic given him by the colonel's wife to wear at the funeral in Richmond. It lacked the impressiveness of the coat's two gleaming rows of brass buttons, but it was less weathered. It also held the colorful insignia of a cavalry major on the cuffs.

He had to inhale in order to fasten his trousers. They'd been trailored for a sixteen-year-old boy, not a man of twenty. The tunic fit better. As a final measure he wiped the dust and grit from his broad, black saber belt and fastened it to his side. Then he added the blue sash distinctive of the Texas cavalry.

He dabbed his cheeks lightly with lilac water, then stood aside when the servants he had summoned reappeared to take away the tub. A frail girl of fourteen or so came up to take his dirty clothes to be washed. She shook her head at the stockings.

"Miz Delamer's got herself some fresh rags, sure as ever," the girl said, mumbling over and over to herself as she left with the clothes.

Willie sat down beside the trunk a moment, looking over the reminders of a part of his life that had passed. The saber he'd taken off the Ohio colonel at Five Forks was there. Three pistols and a Sharps carbine lay in oiled rags; he'd heard the Yanks were disarming the countryside, and so he'd brought them home with him. And there were the sketches of battlefields made by young Danny Nolan before a cannon ball had found him at Petersburg.

Most treasured of all was the blue silk flag with the bright silver star in the center. Around the base of the star were two laurel branches. It was the flag his father had taken to Shiloh. Willie'd carried it from there to Virginia.

"Willie, dinner's ready to be served," James whispered to him from the doorway. "Would you like yours brought to you?"

"No, I'm almost ready, James," he said. "You suppose you could spare a pair of stockings?"

24

"Surely," James said, entering the room and opening a drawer in one of the chests. "Here," he said, handing the stockings to his brother.

"Thanks," Willie said, sitting on the bed and putting on the stockings.

"What's this, Willie?" James asked, pointing to the flag.

"The battle flag of the Second Texas Infantry," Willie explained. "I adopted it as the banner of the Comanche Raiders, my squadron of cavalry up in Virginia."

"It's got stains on it," James said, pointing to the deep brown spatters near the bottom of the flag.

"Blood," Willie said casually. "Flag bearers made good targets for sharpshooters. We lost seven in one charge back in the Valley. We were detached to Early's command. That was when Sheridan took to burning the farms. Peaceful women and children near starved after that. James, if you could've seen the way the earth was blackened, the cattle and hogs and chickens all shot to pieces. That's the face of war."

"We'd best get down to dinner," James said, nudging Willie's shoulder.

"Yes, it would seem the thing to do," Willie agreed, following James out the room.

CHAPTER 4

Ψ

Washed and clean-shaven, Major Willie Delamer cut a dashing figure. Even Matthew, who'd thought Mr. Sam's long lost brother a bit coarse for such a fine family, admitted the man was handsome in a manner.

James was especially taken with the change. It seemed his brother had truly returned. After dinner James took it upon himself to lead Willie around the house and the ranch, introducing his brother to servants and ranch hands alike.

Willie's sharp mind took it all in. He observed every detail of life on the Trident Ranch. The Negroes that took care of the house were all related, Matthew's mother and three sisters. Two white men of doubtful character tended the garden and did what heavy work was required about the house. The stable was looked after by old Ben Sawyer, a blacksmith Bill Delamer had brought out from Austin. Ben's boys saw to the horses. They were the only ones Willie felt at ease around.

There were close to three thousand head of cattle on the ranch. More were strewn along the unfenced range to the south. Hundreds of horses, too. The ranch was certainly not wanting for stock.

What worried Willie was the strange something that no one ever said to him. Some of the hands had worked for his father. Others had fought in the Second Texas until the regiment surrendered at Vicksburg. They all shook Willie's hand and welcomed him back. But no one would talk about Sam or the ranch.

It was near sundown when Willie and James drove their wagon back toward the house. They crossed the river pasture and rolled along the road past the charred remains of the old white house. As they topped the hill, Willie shouted to stop. He then jumped down from the wagon and stared back down the hill.

"Willie?" James asked, pulling the wagon to a halt.

"What happened to the Treaty Oak?" Willie shouted, fire in his eyes. "Somebody cut it!"

James walked to his side and looked at the stump of a great white oak tree. Beside the stump lay three great lengths of tree trunk, each thrown in a different direction.

"Who did that?" Willie asked.

"Comanches," James said. "Close to three months after you and Papa rode out. They started raiding a week or so later. They burned half the valley."

"Why?" Willie asked.

"Who knows?" James asked, shrugging his shoulders. "I don't suppose it matters."

"It matters to me!" Willie said, his eyes turning cold and hard so that James's knees began to shake.

"Sam says old Yellow Shirt took a fever and died. His son chopped down the tree and went wild, killing and burning. I heard from someone else that it was because the rest of the tribe was growing restless. Nobody knows for sure. I do know Yellow Shirt died. They buried him up there."

James pointed to the top of the cliffs across the river.

"Maybe Red Wolf had a vision," Willie said, sitting on a nearby boulder. "It must have been strong medicine to make him cut down the oak. That cursed Yellow Shirt's

27

soul for sure. It was his pledge that there be peace between his people and ours."

"It was a broken promise," James said angrily. "The Comanches hit our place three times. The first time it was all we could do to get out alive. I was nearly scalped, and little Charlie, Sam's second boy, caught an arrow in the chest. He's buried on the hill with Mama and Papa."

"So now the Comanches are gone, too?"

"They still raid our stock some, but Sam hit them hard after Charlie died, killed off the worst of them. Red Wolf's got a village out past Jaster's Mountain, or so they say. But most of the Comanches have crossed the Red River."

"I think I'd like to go up and pray by Yellow Shirt's grave tonight, James. I guess it's been too long since I've done any praying."

"There's nothing up there anymore," James said. "Sam had every last bit of it torn down. The old chief's carcass was thrown in the river."

"What?" Willie said, rising to his feet. "He didn't touch the old scaffolds? Not the village of the ancient ones?"

"Sam tore it down, every bit of it. He said he didn't want any reminders of Indians on his land."

"He had no right," Willie said with hatred in his voice. "It was always understood that place was mine. It was a sacred place, a cemetery. It's a crime to disturb the resting place of the dead."

"That's all hogwash," James said, laughing. "Like the stories you used to tell me about buffalo women and she-devils."

"When you've been out there all alone you'll know there's more to it than that, James. There's something up there with power. And it'll be angry over what Sam's done."

"Sure, Willie," James said, smiling. "It's why Mama and Papa died, why the Yanks have come with their taxes and new laws."

James expected Willie to echo his laughter, but there was nothing humorous about Willie's face. A stern expression covered that face, and rage filled the dark eyes dangerously.

"There's nothing you can do about it now, Willie," James said, trying to calm his brother. "It's done. Sam didn't do it to spite you. He was hurt and angry because they'd killed little Charlie. Try to understand."

Willie sighed. He did understand how a man felt who'd lost someone he loved. He understood death better than most. Nearly everyone he'd trusted, loved, relied on had died.

"You want to stop and pay your respects to Mama?" James asked. "The plot's just up the hill a way."

"Yes," Willie said, walking back to the wagon. "I know where it is."

But though Willie knew the spot, he wouldn't have recognized it. The knoll was surrounded by an iron fence. A large gate with tall spikes stood on one side. Stamped in black lettering on a thin iron plate over the gate was the name DELAMER. On each side of the name was a small trident, the same mark that was stamped on everything else.

Willie walked through the gate, reminded of the cemetery in Richmond where they'd buried the colonel. Inside the iron fence were five identical granite headstones. On each a name had been etched. Dates of birth and death were there, too. Near the top of each stone was a small circle with a trident in the center.

"Branded, just like a cow," Willie said under his breath.

The first stone was for his father. COLONEL BILL DELAMER, HERO AND PATRIOT, it read.

"Papa," Willie spoke softly, touching the cold edge of the monument. "I'll keep my promise, Papa."

James had entered the plot by then. Willie could feel his brother close to him. Glancing back, he thought he spotted tears in the eyes of the young man.

Their mother was next in line. ELIZABETH THOMPSON DELAMER, FIRST LADY OF THE TRIDENT RANCH. Willie remembered the softness of her side, the warmth of her touch. She hadn't wanted him to ride off to war. And if he'd stayed, maybe she wouldn't be lying there in the cold earth.

Willie could hear James crying. It was not unmanly to

cry for someone so loved as a mother, yet Willie shed no tears. His crying was done inside, where it didn't show. It had been years since tears had trickled down his cheeks.

Willie moved along the line of tombstones. There was one for Christine, the little sister who'd been stillborn two winters after Willie'd been born. Then came Stephen, the brother who would have been twelve that summer. Finally he paused beside the stone that marked the grave of little Charlie. CHARLES DELAMER, BELOVED SON, the inscription read.

Willie knelt and touched the monument. In his silent way he shed a tear for the nephew he'd never known. Then he got to his feet and walked past the gate.

Willie wasn't pleased with the changes he'd seen. Gone were the Comanches, the Treaty Oak. Gone was the village of the ancient ones, that strange tie to the past that filled Willie with an awe of things greater than mere men.

He disliked the cemetery, too. There was something cold and unfeeling about stone and iron. And it was a place that would be filled by other stones, other graves. He liked it better when there were just the two simple wooden crosses beneath the tall white oaks.

"I guess we'd better head for home," James spoke from the graveyard. "Sam'll probably be waiting."

"Yes, and I've got a lot . . . I'm eager to see him again."

Willie frowned. He'd almost said it. There were a lot of things Sam would have to explain, a lot of answers Willie had coming.

When they were seated together on the seat of the wagon, James turned to his brother.

"I'm sorry I started crying, Willie. I fight it, but I usually break down and make a fool of myself."

"I didn't notice," Willie said.

Willie wanted to reach out to his brother then, provide some comfort. But there was nothing within him to give. His eyes were cold, and his heart had grown hard.

CHAPTER 5

Ψ

Sam Houston Delamer had been named for the general who'd won Texas her independence at San Jacinto some thirty years before. He wore the name proudly, boasting any man bearing the names of two great Texas patriots could hardly be an ordinary man.

Sam Delamer was an imposing figure. He stood six feet tall and carried two hundred hardened pounds on a solid frame. His dark hair and heavy eyebrows gave him an almost sinister look which he used to advantage in business dealings. A heavy black moustache curled around his upper lip so that when he smiled, he took on a somewhat satanic appearance.

That evening he rode the tall white stallion purchased from old Jed Greenwood a fortnight earlier. The horse could have run all the way to Mexico, but Sam held him to a steady trot. Horsemanship had never been one of his talents, and being thrown twice at Elkhorn Tavern had convinced him the cavalry should be left to others.

It proved a useful decision. He could proudly point to

his captain's commission when speaking to natives of the valley. And in dealing with representatives of the federals at Fort Belknap he was always quick to point out his fighting had mainly been directed against the Comanches.

At Sam's side rolled a small carriage. Inside sat Judge DeWitt Fulton. The judge, as he was known along the Brazos, held the title through no great legal expertise. In point of fact the man had seen more of a courtroom from the defendant's chair than from behind the bench.

DeWitt Fulton had arrived the previous fall in Palo Pinto with an appointment from the United States Senate engineered by his former business partner, Senator Ballard of Ohio. The man came equipped with a change of clothes and a franking privilege granted by Congress, all packed inside the notorious carpetbag from which the representatives of the federal reconstruction took their name.

Carpetbaggers. It was a word muttered with contempt in the South. But it was a word which might well spell fortune or bankruptcy to a rancher like Sam Delamer. Judge Fulton controlled all tax levies, administered all laws, decided all disputes. In the year since Appomattox the judge and his companion, Major Winthrop, had enabled the Trident Ranch to grow and prosper.

That night the three men were contemplating one of Helen's lavish dinners. Silverware and fine china already graced a long table in the formal dining room. The fifty-six candles of the crystal chandelier had been lighted.

The cooks had been working all afternoon to prepare a meal of chicken and fishes, boiled and sauteed to suit even the cultured palate of a New Orleans gentleman.

Unlike his brother Willie, Sam Delamer's education had taken place in the drawing rooms and academies of New Orleans. The eldest of the Delamers spoke fluent French and Spanish, could quote Shakespeare and Milton, knew the common statutes of the state of Texas from cover to cover.

The man was both feared and admired throughout the valley, and hated by some. It was Sam Delamer's dream to

32

control the seven counties that lined the Upper Brazos, to dominate an area as immense and wealthy as whole eastern states. In the back of his mind he imagined that one day he, or at least his son Robert, would sit in the capitol as governor of the state.

Who held better claim to such dreams? Wasn't it Sam who'd returned from his brief stint of soldiering to find the ranch in ruins, stock run off, house burned, small son murdered? Wasn't it Sam who'd ridden down the Comanches, carried the war to them so that his name was uttered with the same dread as any of the Indian devil monsters of legend? Wasn't it Sam who'd demanded gold as payment when his neighbors accepted the worthless paper money printed by the secessionist government in Richmond?

Some might have called Sam unpatriotic at the time, but few called him foolish. Now he alone of all the ranchers in the valley was buying land, increasing his herds, contracting beef to the federals. He alone had the funds to build a great house and bring fine furniture and servants from New Orleans where gentlemen were selling their possessions for a song.

Sam disliked the men in the carriage beside him, so much so that he'd ridden the twenty miles from Palo Pinto on horseback. He had no objection to the use they made of their power; it was good business to take advantage of the opportunities life presented. But to steal and plunder the valley in the name of idealism sickened Sam. Whatever the people might say of Sam Delamer, they could never claim he acted behind anyone's back.

When the three men arrived at the house, they were led by Matthew to the rooms upstairs where they might refresh themselves from their journey. Baths were made ready, and fine cigars made of Carolina tobacco were distributed. The small cavalry detachment which followed from Fort Belknap tended their horses and enjoyed lemonade brought to them by young Robert, Sam's eldest.

Sam smiled and swapped stories with the houseguests. He was unusually cheerful. The judge had already granted a permit which would allow the damming of two small creeks on Delamer land. The water wasn't needed for irrigation as Sam had claimed in his petition. But without it two small farms that bordered the Trident Ranch would dry up and blow away.

The smile on Sam's face was in response to this latest triumph. It meant another four hundred acres of Delamer land, sooner or later. There'd be no other offer to buy than the one Sam would propose.

Sam's good mood was such that Helen was unable to distract him. She was trying to tell him something about James. Where was his younger brother anyway? The young man was showing someone around the ranch, a girl probably. James had been riding with the Wood girl lately. Nothing serious, of course; James was young, and he knew better than to consider marrying a farm girl. Not if he planned to read for the law.

They were seated at the table and enjoying a second glass of wine when Helen finally whispered the news.

"Willie's back," she said.

Sam tried not to let the paleness of his face reveal the surprise he felt.

"Bad news?" the judge asked, filling his glass from the decanter.

"Oh, just something to do with the ranch," Sam said, stifling a cough. "Times have been hard of late."

"So you tell us," Major Winthrop said. "Still, you don't seem to be suffering from it." The major waved his hand through the air to indicate the finery all around them.

"Actually, Sam's brother has come home," Helen said, breaking the tension that had come to fill the room. "He was in the army."

"An older brother?" the judge asked, smiling at the thought of a new and less shrewd Delamer to bargain with.

"Younger by five years," Sam said, the smile fading from his face. "He's quite unlike me, as you'll see. Willie grew up with the Indians. He's a fine horseman, but totally lacking in business sense. That's why Papa left the ranch to me alone."

"A wise precaution," Judge Fulton said. "Otherwise the young man might claim a large portion of your holdings."

"You say he was away to war," Major Winthrop said, interrupting. "Most of the men in the valley were at Vicksburg, gave it up and came home."

"Willie was wounded at Shiloh," Sam said, reluctantly relating the military exploits of the brother he'd never liked. "We heard he rode with some cavalrymen to Virginia to fight with Hood. Personally I thought he was dead."

"I'm certain you are relieved that he was not," the judge said, studying Sam's reaction.

"Quite pleased, and grateful to God," Helen said, passing the wine around again.

"I hope he's not one of those rebels who can't admit the war's over," Major Winthrop said. "If they'd put old Sam Grant at the reins a year earlier, we'd've fixed Lee at Chancellorsville. All it took was a man with guts, one who didn't get a weak stomach reading casualty reports."

Sam coughed, then gestured to Matthew. The black man withdrew, then returned with the first course of dinner.

"Aren't we waiting for James?" Helen asked.

"It's been a long day, dear," Sam said.

The table grew quiet as the food was apportioned generously onto the plates. Sam sighed in relief. That fool Winthrop would have spoiled the evening with another of his harangues on how poorly the war had been waged. Helen would have become angry, and an argument would surely have followed.

"Actually I think Willie's quite relieved the war is over, gentlemen," Helen said. "I trust you'll find he's put aside his sword."

"I hope so, ma'am," the major said, abandoning his earlier thoughts as he gazed into the deep blue eyes of his hostess.

"How soon do you expect to buy the two properties we discussed?" Judge Fulton asked Sam. "By the end of the month?"

"I would expect," Sam said. "The Longs are ready right

now. It's only those others, the Raymonds, that have been fighting it. Doesn't do any good to have the one place without the other."

"You add those two farms and the Cobbs will be cut off," the judge said. "That's the pearl you're really after."

Sam tried to hide his anger. It was not good that the judge had seen through his tactics.

"Why, Judge," Helen said, blushing, "Arthur Cobb was Bill Delamer's closest friend. His son Travis and Willie served together in the war."

"Oh?" the judge said, a smile curling his lips. "My compliments . . . for the meal, ma'am."

But it was to Sam that the man nodded, and everyone understood the judge's admiration was reserved for the man who'd cut the throat of a friend for the sake of business.

As the four of them shared the unspoken truth, the front doors swung open, and the sound of heavy boots on the floorboards broke their attention.

"Oh, my God," Sam said, rising as Willie, fully adorned in Confederate gray and cavalry saber, entered the house.

"Dear me," Helen said, raising her handkerchief to her lips.

"Well," the judge said, starting toward the two younger Delamer brothers as they approached.

"Dirty reb," Major Winthrop said, unfastening the snap on the holster of his revolver.

"Gentlemen, allow me to introduce my brother, William Delamer III," Sam said, racing around the table to intercept Willie before the judge got there.

"Judge DeWitt Fulton," the judge said, shaking Willie's hand. "And this is Major Marcus Winthrop, adjutant commander of Fort Belknap."

Willie turned toward the major and stared. They'd met before, he was sure of it.

"What happened to old Judge Taylor?" Willie asked, shaking Sam's sweaty hand.

"Retired to his daughter's land down in the hill country," Sam explained.

"All Confederate appointees were removed from positions of authority," the major said.

"Judge Taylor was holding court when nobody lived out here but rattlesnakes and polecats," Willie said. "He came out with Papa when the Comanches still controlled the valley. His title came from President Houston in the old Republic days."

"Well, he's gone now, Willie," Sam said, leading his brothers to the table. "I expect you're hungry and have better things to do with your mouths than fill them with idle chatter."

Willie read his older brother's eyes. It was clear that these were men not to be talked around. James sat beside him at the end of the table where places had been left for them, and Matthew soon appeared with more food.

"Have we met before?" the major asked Willie.

"It doesn't seem likely," Willie said, his eyes watering as the chicken melted in his mouth.

"Maybe not, but I don't forget a face. I've seen you before."

"Probably in the war," Judge Fulton said, sipping a fifth glass of wine. "You two were on opposite sides of that unpleasantness, in case you've forgotten."

"It's best forgotten," Sam said, trying to close the subject.

"I remember now," the major said. "The Wilderness. We were after Longstreet. Cagey old devil'd just disappeared in the woods. I led my company across an open field. Just as we met the tail end of the reb line, we were hit from the flank by that bunch of Texans. Big blue flag and all. You were there, you and some colonel with a big red moustache."

"You left your whole line exposed," Willie said, ignoring a warning glance from Sam. "It was just like the colonel expected. You charged the infantry. We came in and pushed you right into our riflemen. We must have cut down two hundred men that afternoon."

"Yes," the major said, his eyes red with hatred. "Two of those men were my brothers. I swore I'd see you all in hell for that."

"Well, we mostly are," Willie said, laughing. "Hell or Texas."

The humor didn't catch on. Helen managed a laugh, but the others stared at the major. He stood up, his fingers reaching for a pistol.

"Put that gun down, Winthrop!" the judge commanded. "You're a guest in this house. Go outside and get some air."

The major stalked off, pausing to give Willie a look that promised violence. James shivered, and even Sam seemed stunned. Willie just went on eating his dinner.

"The chicken is marvelous, Helen," Willie said. "I hope you'll pass on my compliments to the cooks."

"Surely," Helen said, her face still white from the shock of having a pistol drawn at her dinner table.

"You must excuse Major Winthrop, Sam," the judge said, his speech growing slightly slurred. "He's got a bit of a temper."

"I understand," Sam said, gesturing to Willie.

"I hope you weren't addressing those remarks to me, sir," Willie said, surprising them all with the formality of his speech. "I'm accustomed to seeing revolvers pointed in my direction. And I understand how a man feels who's lost friends to the enemy." For a moment the chill flashed through Willie's eyes. It was only there a moment, though. Then the eyes reclaimed the brightness they'd held all through dinner.

James and Willie quietly ate the last of their dinner, and the servants removed the plates. Fresh blackberry pie was served for dessert, and a final round of wine passed around the table.

After dinner Sam went out to find the major and mend the break in their relationship. James set off to find the letter Mary had left for Willie. The judge took Willie aside, his breath heavy with wine and food.

"Your brother didn't seem so pleased to see you," the man said to Willie.

"He was preoccupied," Willie said, realizing the judge was not nearly so drunk as he was pretending.

"Sam Delamer's a man to watch, boy," the judge said, smiling in a way that reminded Willie of a rattlesnake. "I wouldn't go turning my back to him. As for Winthrop, I'd swap that uniform for some homespun. Make it blue, too."

"I'll consider it," Willie said.

"You really fight with Lee?"

"From the summer of '62 on."

"All you rebs got ice in your bellies? Must be what took so long. Must be."

Willie smiled at the man. He was obviously performing.

"You remember, though," the judge said, clutching Willie's arm so that it was clear the words were serious. "You remember you ain't riding with Jeb Stuart now, boy. You're in Judge DeWitt Fulton's district. And here I'm law and court. I can make a man or I can hang him."

The judge then staggered toward the stairs, headed for the guest room. Willie felt the oppressive heat inside the house and headed for the door. It was dark outside, and as cool as it ever got in Texas during the spring. He wiped his forehead, surprised that he wasn't perspiring.

CHAPTER 6

Ψ

Anyone else would have known it was a mistake to walk toward the barn. That was where the cavalry escort was. Still full of rage, Major Marcus Winthrop had sought the one audience that couldn't refuse to listen. As the men nodded and echoed his outrage that a reb officer who'd ridden with Lee should still have a saber at his hip, that same officer stood in the moonlight not thirty yards away.

Willie was staring at the stars overhead, feeling good that at least stars stayed the same. He didn't notice the man across from him pointing and shouting to his companions. It was only when a bullet struck the ground beside his foot that his attention was drawn.

The major hadn't intended to miss. The pistol was aimed for Willie's forehead. But Marcus Winthrop had never been the best of marksmen, and there was the wine to figure in as well.

The pistol shot stirred someone in the barn, and shouts could be heard inside the house. The federal officer fired a second time, nicking the toe of Willie's left boot.

By that time the whole courtyard was alive with activity. The other soldiers gasped and stared as their commander fired a third time at the defenseless Confederate. The bullet might have found a target had not Willie rolled to his right.

The men were further filled with horror as the man in gray took out a long Colt revolver and fired at his would-be assassin. Major Marcus Winthrop coughed once, then turned to one side. Bright red blood trickled from the man's lip. Then he fell, a single round hole filling the center of his chest.

The cavalrymen raced to where Willie lay, arms at his sides, blood dribbling from the hole in his foot. The men stripped him of his pistol and saber, then forced him to his feet. As they argued over what had happened, Judge Fulton stepped out of the house, his face white and sober.

"Leave the boy be," he told the soldiers. "He was only acting in self-defense."

A look of relief filled Willie's eyes, and he accepted his weapons from the soldiers without emotion.

"What happened?" Sam asked, racing out into the court-yard.

"Your brother just shot an officer of the United States Army," Judge Fulton said, pointing to Willie.

"My God," Sam said, staring at Winthrop's corpse. "I suppose you'll have to take him to the fort for trial."

"No, nothing so formal as that," the judge said. "Likely there'll just be a small fine. And we may have to reappraise the worth of your property. We'll discuss it over breakfast."

When the judge looked in Willie's direction, he found himself staring into eyes that understood perfectly. Judge Fulton's sole concern was how to make the most of the opportunity before him.

"Might be a good idea for you to spend some time in the hills, son," the judge said. "You're a mite quick with your hands for my comfort."

"I can see how you might be a little nervous," Willie said, taking a long time to replace his pistol in its holster.

41

"I don't see why any fine should be paid by a man for defending himself."

"Oh, call it a new ordinance," Judge Fulton said, laughing. "Fine for carrying a cavalry saber within the bounds of Palo Pinto County."

"You can't fine a man for violating a law before it was on the books," Willie said, surprising the judge with a knowledge of the law.

"Oh, Mr. Delamer, you're mistaken. The law is on my books. You'll find it there if you'd care to look for it tomorrow morning."

"I'm sure," Willie said, frowning.

"Leave it," James said, grabbing Willie's hand. "It's the way things work around here."

"It's not right," Willie said, staring at his younger brother.

"Maybe, but we've got the money. Law or no law, Sam would have paid him the same for whatever reason. The judge could just as easily levy a fence tax or a water usage fee. He's done it before."

"And this happens regular?"

"Sure," James said, annoyed at Willie's lack of understanding.

Willie turned and walked away, muttering to himself.

"Things always change, Papa," he said, unbuckling his gunbelt. "But not for the best."

"Willie!" Sam called from the doorway. "This isn't settled!"

"Then let's settle it!" Willie yelled, a cold stare filling his face so that even Sam flinched.

The two brothers reentered the house, passing Judge Fulton on their way down the main hall to a room Willie had not yet seen. Sam waved his brother inside, then closed the heavy oak door.

The two men faced each other across a large desk. Sam sat behind it, rummaging through papers to break the silence. He finally found something and looked up at Willie.

"James took you around today," Sam said, pausing.

Willie stared straight ahead.

"I'll take that for a Yes. You can see we've made a lot of changes. I've tripled the acreage. Now we run thousands of head of cattle. Since the end of war we've made over ten thousand dollars. After Judge Fulton's taxes."

"I wouldn't know about that," Willie said.

"Of course you wouldn't," Sam said, putting on his business smile. "But you will. The judge is going to make his fortune with or without us. By scratching his back we're able to do business pretty much as we choose."

"How?"

"Oh, he's made a few judgments that, shall we say, didn't hurt the Trident Ranch."

"I see," Willie said.

"I really don't see why you're so angry," Sam said, shaking his head. "Papa used to buy off old Judge Taylor."

"What started the Comanche war?"

"The Comanche war? You're asking me? Well, little brother, it wasn't me! I raised a cavalry company and headed up to Little Rock. We fought the Yanks at Elkhorn Tavern."

"And you came home."

"And I came home. Look, Willie, I'm no Bill Delamer. I won't go riding off to battle every other week. I was never cut out to be a soldier. Papa knew that. He sent me to school so I'd know how to manage things."

"And you've certainly done that," Willie said, sneering.

"Yes, and I'll continue to. Before my sons are grown, I'll control this whole valley, both sides of the river for as far as I care to. People will see that trident on a cow's rump and know the Delamers have come that way."

"And what about the old ways? What about the ancient ones? James said you tore down all the scaffolds."

"So that's it," Sam said, smiling. It was the businessman in him. He'd found his opponent's weak spot, his vulnerability.

"What did it gain you, Sam? The land up there's not good for anything!"

"No good at all, Willie," Sam said, turning his face away in pretended remorse. "I was angry, pure and simple. They'd

43

killed little Charlie. You didn't even know the boy, but he was a lot like you, free and full of fire. He could run like the wind, and he wasn't but a tadpole. I swore they'd pay."

"Wasn't it enough to fight them? Did you have to defile the cliff? Did you really dump Yellow Shirt's body in the river? He was an honorable man, Sam, Papa's sworn friend."

"It was a terrible thing, Willie. But I was crazy with grief. It's all I can tell you."

Willie frowned. There would be no arguing. Sam just nodded at everything that was said. Willie could have stood up and fought it out, hit hard with every ounce of strength he had. But all he could manage was understanding for the grief Sam described. Grief was something Willie knew too well.

"I'm sorry I was angry," Willie finally said, the hardness in his eyes fading. "I've had a long ride back from Virginia. We were shot at and robbed more times than I'd care to remember. I brought one boy, just seventeen, all the way from Appomattox only to see him shot from ambush at the Trinity River crossing.

"I haven't thought of anything but coming home for five years. I've bled over hills and rivers from Tennessee to Pennsylvania. Then I got here and found Mama dead, James changed, the Indians gone. You know what I saw before anything else when I got here? Fences!

"You saw how it was tonight. That Yank major shot three bullets at me. If he'd had a little less liquor inside him or a steadier hand, I'd be lying out there instead of him. And that judge of yours would be thinking up a burying tax."

Sam laughed at that, but no smile crossed Willie's lips.

"I'm glad you're enjoying this, Sam, because I don't think there'll be many smiles in the days to come. I thought I'd left the war behind in Virginia, but it seems like it followed me back."

"There'll always be a war to be fought in this valley," Sam said, walking over to a large map on the north wall of the room. "Look here. The river runs through our holdings, but we don't control the whole thing. There's a big stretch

44

to the east and another to the west. We've got most of the north bank. Now it's time to go after the other."

"What are you talking about?" Willie asked, staring at the map. "That land belongs to our neighbors, people who settled here when Papa made the treaty with Yellow Shirt."

"That was a long time ago."

Willie turned away and examined the rest of the room. There was a portrait of Sam done a few years earlier. A smaller one of Helen stood beside it. Over a great fireplace hung a long sword with a jeweled handle. Willie had held that sword twice—once after returning from his six-week stay in the camps of the Comanches. The other time had been when his father had explained about the sword before leaving for the war.

"This sword was given to my grandfather by the king of France, Willie. They called him the Chevalier de Lyon. When the revolution came, that sword cost him his home, his position in the army, everything. He was barely able to get aboard a ship bound for New Orleans.

"Whenever I get tired or seem to lose my way, I look at that sword. It reminds me that my grandfather came to this continent with nothing. Nothing but a name he gave himself and a sword that reminded him the king of France once shook his hand.

"We're Delamers, Willie, and we don't bow to anyone. We sometimes sacrifice the best we have in this world, give it up so our children can have it better. My father died at Goliad so that I could be free. And if it comes to pass that I die in this war, then it's so that you and your children will also be free."

Free? Willie asked himself if they were free. He doubted it.

"You're back in Virginia, aren't you?" Sam asked. "Well, I shouldn't be surprised. You've come a long way, and tonight hasn't been any party. You rest some. I'll send Matthew up with some cloth to bandage your foot. It's not serious, is it?"

"No."

"And here. I've got a letter for you that Mary left. She's gone to . . ."

"Colorado," Willie said, taking the letter. "James told me about it."

"Tomorrow it'd be best if you rode out to the old line shack by the southern boundary. Take Henry King. You can check the fences there for gaps. You might leave early."

"I'm used to early sunrises, Sam. Be sure to pay my respects to the judge."

There was a scowl on Willie's face as he left, and Sam took note of it. It would do no harm to have Willie out of the house before the judge had a chance to arouse any angry responses. Willie was a little dangerous.

By the time Willie reached the room he was to share with James that night, Matthew had already gathered the bandages and some ointment. Treating the wound was nothing for a man of Willie's experiences. Mending the boot took longer than the hole in his foot.

By the light of a single candle Willie read the letter. The only sound in the room was the quiet breathing of James in the next bed. Shed of his fancy clothes, Willie's brother seemed smaller, more of a boy. Willie remembered the child who'd once sat on his lap and listened to stories of Indians and devils. But as he undressed, Willie knew that could never be again. That much was clear even before he read Mary's letter.

CHAPTER 7

Willie rode the southern boundary of the ranch that morning, observing the familiar creeks and rocks and hills. No smile appeared on his face as he passed three small houses which had once belonged to close friends of his father.

Old Henry King plodded along at Willie's side, humming range songs and answering questions.

"Yup, they been gone most o' two years now," Henry said as they rode past the old Ferguson place. "Comanches hit the farms hereabouts hard."

But when Willie probed for an answer to why Sam had begun stringing the fences, Henry started talking about some old deer hunt he'd gone on. Later the ranch hand retold the history of the war Bill Delamer had fought against Yellow Shirt and his band of Indians.

He's an old man now, Willie thought to himself. There's gray in his beard, and that fall he took from Fireball ten years ago's made him lame.

Everything's changed. That was what Mary'd written.

"One morning I looked across the valley and found it wasn't home anymore."

He knew the feeling. Even the cliffs, the high places where the ancient ones had built their village, had been taken away from him. That tie he felt to the land, the pull which had drawn him back across two thousand miles had been cut in one terrible day. And the softness of his mother, the understanding of his sister had vanished like a wisp of a cloud on a Texas summer day.

"Build the ranch, Willie," his father had said.

"It's built, Papa," Willie mumbled in a voice so low Henry couldn't hear. "But it's not like you intended."

"You say something, son?" Henry asked.

"No, just remembering," Willie said. "You ever ride out to the Cobb place?"

"Can't say as I do," Henry said. "Got trouble enough watchin' the Trident lands."

"Well, I'll leave you to them, Henry," Willie said. "I promised Trav to drop by and pay my respects."

"You watch yourself out there, boy," Henry said, nervously pulling his horse to a halt. "Could be you're not welcome."

"Not welcome?" Willie asked, a smile coming to his face. "I'd better be."

Giving old Henry a parting nod, Willie spurred Thunder and started toward a rise that led the way to Bluff Creek. Not welcome? Surely Ellen couldn't have changed, too.

Ellen. Even the sound of her name brought warmth to Willie's insides. When he'd left she was but fourteen, more frail girl than woman. But valley girls had a way of growing up fast. If Willie hadn't ridden to war, he and Ellen would be married with a fine little family by now.

Willie reached into his pocket and took out the big gold watch his father had bought him in Houston. Inside was a small cameo of Ellen. The picture had never done her justice, but it had kept him warm through many a lonely night.

Willie closed his eyes and let the memory of her face come back to him. She had beautiful auburn hair, soft like

48

clover on the hillside in springtime. Her skin was pale and delicate, her cheeks full of red as if painted with rose petals. Her nose was small, and her lips were like two fine lines drawn across her mouth by nature's finest artist.

But most of all Willie saw Ellen's eyes. Those eyes were blue as the sky, rich pools of violet that quickened his pulse, made his insides quiver. How he longed to see those eyes, touch those soft hands of hers.

Thunder seemed to sense the new urgency in Willie's movements. The horse stepped faster, moving from a canter to a gallop. Great swirls of dust sprang up behind him, marking his passage. Soon Willie would see Ellen again. Everything else seemed minor, unimportant.

It took no more than half an hour to cover the distance to the Cobb farm. Willie felt himself at home in the saddle, and he relaxed as the powerful horse took each rise of ground in stride. He wished he hadn't let James talk him out of wearing the uniform. The trousers and homespun shirt he wore made him seem like an ordinary ranch hand. Only the gray hat remained of the Confederate major he'd been a year before.

The uniform would have angered the cavalrymen, though. James was right about that. It certainly wouldn't have helped with the judge, either. As Willie began growing angry once more at the way Sam went along with that crooked politician, the gate to the Cobb farm appeared, and he remembered Ellen's eyes again.

He slowed his horse to a trot and nervously rode through the gate. He was suddenly unsure of himself. He'd had no news of Ellen in two and a half years. Perhaps she'd married. For all he knew she could be dead. Or maybe she might find that he'd changed too much.

No, Willie told himself. Life couldn't be that cruel. Ellen was all he had left of the old world, left behind that autumn of '61. She had to be waiting for him.

Willie slid down from the saddle and tied his horse to the small hitching rack in front of the house. The farmyard was deserted. Likely the men were in the fields. Willie walked to the door and knocked lightly on the wooden frame. A moment later he heard footsteps.

He hoped it would be Ellen. Oh, how he hungered for the sight of her. But it wasn't Ellen, or Travis, either, who met Willie. It was Arthur Cobb, the old veteran of San Jacinto who'd first ridden to the Brazos with Willie's father.

For several minutes the man stared at Willie. Art Cobb chomped on a plug of chewing tobacco, examining every inch of the man Willie had become.

"This is the Cobb place," the man finally said. "You got business here?"

"Mr. Cobb, I'm Willie Delamer," Willie said, taking off his hat. "Trav invited me to supper, and I was hoping to see Ellen."

"She's out to market with her ma," Mr. Cobb said, not a hint of friendship in his voice.

"Could I wait for her?" Willie asked, puzzled that the man who'd been his father's best friend had not invited him inside.

"Just as soon you wouldn't," the man said. "There's nothing here for you, Willie Delamer."

"Sir?" Willie asked, surprised that Arthur Cobb would close the door in his face.

"I won't turn you away, boy, since you wore the Confederate gray alongside my own Travis. But you might as well know that I got no use for Delamers."

"I don't understand," Willie said, scratching his head. "Did I say something wrong? Is Ellen pledged to somebody else?"

The man's frown passed away. The door swung open, and Mr. Cobb walked out onto the porch. The man pointed Willie to a chair, then sat down beside him.

"Best thing in this world for Ellen would've been you takin' a musket ball at Shiloh like your pa. She's spent five years now pinin' and frettin' over a man that can never bring her nothin' but grief. That's you, Willie."

"Me?"

"When your pa and me first come to this valley, all we

saw was injuns and junipers. Then this cussed critter grew up right out of the Brazos. They call it a Delamer. I seen enough of 'em to stay clear. They smile and take you with the hand of friendship, then hit your behind like a rattler.

"I got great sorrow in my heart your pa ever had himself a son. I got a lot of affection for that sister of yours and her man, but I can't abide Sam or that pup James, neither."

Willie leaned back and stared at the bright afternoon sun. It was hot, and sweat flowed across his forehead and down his neck.

"Tell me about it," Willie said. "I've asked everybody else. If there's been wrong done, I'll see it's made right."

Art Cobb laughed, then slapped Willie's knee.

"You really don't know, do you, boy?"

"Know what?" Willie asked, his face growing crimson. "What's been happening in this valley?"

"You been a good friend to my boy, Willie Delamer, so I can't bring myself to say it all. But your brother is no better'n a liar and a cheat. He rides over to Palo Pinto or Jacksboro once a week to do business with that Yank judge and his friendly cavalry major. Next thing you know another farm gets itself swallowed up by them blamed fences of his.

"I got a powerful hatred for that brother of yours, boy. I stood there when we buried your pa and listened to him say how one day the Trident brand would be stamped on every tree and cow for a hundred miles. Your pa never meant that ranch to grow at the expense of his friends. Bill Delamer'd give a hundred acres to any man who'd pick up a rifle and fight Comanches. Many's the winter he'd bring us fresh meat when I was down with a fever. He was a good man."

"The best," Willie said.

"But that Sam's got no feel for the land. I figure he'll own all seven counties in this valley 'fore they lay him out. Never'll belong here, though. The hills know a man's heart."

"Part of that ranch belongs to me," Willie said, his eyes cold. "I mean to have the cliffs for sure. Maybe the south

51

bank of the river. I know Papa intended it should be that way."

"Willie, Bill planned you should run the whole spread," Mr. Cobb said. "He told old Yellow Shirt you and Red Wolf'd make the peace last another lifetime. But nobody could find it put down on paper, and you was gone. Old Judge Taylor might've split things up, but not this Yank Fulton. He's out to own us all. Worse than Sam."

"So what do I do?" Willie asked.

"You got it easy, Willie," the man said. "All you do is sit in them fine linen chairs and sip New Orleans brandy. Smile at the fine ladies and shake hands with the judge and his bluecoat major."

"Nobody'll be shakin' hands with that major," Willie said, frowning.

"What?"

"I shot him dead last night. Didn't intend it that way, but the man took to shootin' bullets at me. I didn't fight my way through Tennessee and Virginia to have some Yank major shoot me in my own yard."

"What'd Sam say?" Mr. Cobb asked.

"Told me to ride the south acreage for a time. I expect he'll pay off that judge, and everything will be back to normal."

"Willie, you take care to keep your eyes open," Mr. Cobb told him. "Men in this valley don't do too well if they make things hard on Mr. Sam Delamer."

"I think I'm strong enough to take care of myself," Willie said, standing up. "I can be as hard as rock when there's need."

"There's need," the man said, wiping sweat from his wrinkled forehead.

Their conversation was interrupted by a sound in the distance. Willie followed Mr. Cobb's eyes past the gate to where a wagon was rolling up the market road. On the front seat of the wagon sat Mrs. Arthur Cobb and Willie's old friend Travis. Between them was a thin-faced girl of nineteen, her face lit by sparkling eyes. Sunlight danced across long strands of auburn hair.

"Ellen," Willie mumbled to himself.

He felt something stir inside him as he watched the wagon come closer. In spite of Travis's firm hand at the reins, the horses took an eternity to cover the final hundred yards to the gate. All that while Willie stood frozen in his tracks, unable to advance or retreat.

"Well, you goin' to wait here all day, boy?" Mr. Cobb finally asked, nudging Willie in the ribs.

"No, sir," Willie said, trying to conceal a smile.

Before another word could be spoken, Willie raced to the gate and waited for the wagon to halt.

"Ellen!" he shouted.

She said nothing, just jumped from the wagon and ran into his powerful arms. Her soft hair fell against his cheek, and warmth welled up inside his chest as he held her against him.

"I've missed you," he said, kissing her right there in front of her family.

"Have you?" she asked, her whole face filled with a strange sort of glow. "I prayed every day and every night that you would come back."

"In spite of Sam?"

"Sam be hanged," she said, hugging him around his iron waist. "I didn't pledge myself or anything to Sam."

"You've grown into a fine figure of a woman, Ellen Cobb," Willie said, holding her at arm's length to examine more closely the delicate figure she'd added in his absence.

"And you've lost your boyishness, Willie Delamer," she told him, laughing. "Mostly a man now, I'd say."

"So would a few hundred Yanks," Travis said, leading them both toward the house. "And wait till you taste her fried chicken, Willie. Made special for you, I expect."

Willie paused only long enough to nod to Mrs. Cobb and the little ones. Then he followed Ellen inside the house.

53

CHAPTER 8

Little remained on the outside of the girl Ellen had been. Her speech, her manner was that of a woman. She wasn't old enough to lose the youthfulness in her face, but Willie observed how hard her arms had become, how much stronger her legs were now.

It was the way Texas farm girls were grown. Tough and strong as a white oak tree, his father had once said. Some might not find such a woman to their taste. Willie wouldn't trade Ellen for a room filled with New Orleans debutantes, though.

That afternoon they talked. Talked and talked and talked. They remembered a childhood of chasing each other through the river, racing horses over hillsides, sharing the same sunset on a lonely knoll.

Ellen told him about the Comanche war, about his mother and about Mary and James and Sam. Willie related his exploits in the war, the days he'd lain delirious in Corinth imagining her at his side.

"What has your father so upset?" Willie finally asked.

"Lots of little things," Ellen told him. "The fences that have broken up the range, the way Sam screens off cattle from the river. Mostly Pa worries about the way small farms are getting gobbled up by the Trident."

"I saw Sam's map," Willie said. "He wants the whole valley. But I don't see how he can force you out. Your father's got enough stock and crops to feed the state."

"It's not so hard for Sam," she said, leaning against his shoulder. "Sam keeps buying up the small farms along the market roads. He's practically got us surrounded. Once he strings his wire through here we won't have a way to market. And we rely on the creeks for water. He's gone to damming up the streams elsewhere."

Willie leaned back against the hard wooden back of the chair they shared. He ran over in his mind the words Mary had written: "There was a will, Willie. I saw it. I don't care for myself, and James had been promised money and percentages of the ranch profits. But you . . ."

"What's the matter, Willie?" Ellen asked.

"Nothing," he said. "I was just thinking about something Mary wrote."

"About what?"

"About there being a will."

"Willie, if there was a will, Judge Taylor would know about it. You should ride down there and talk to him about it. At least write."

"Do you suppose Sam would really lie about something like that?" Willie asked.

"He's done worse," Ellen said, scowling.

"Such as?"

"He's your brother, and I won't speak ill of him. But there are people who were given land by Bill Delamer who were run off it by Sam."

"If I write the judge, will you post the letter, Ellen?" Willie asked. "It'd be better if Sam didn't know about it."

"I'll get Travis to take it to town. Not to Palo Pinto, either. That Judge Fulton's got more eyes than you could imagine."

Ellen left for a moment. She returned with paper, pen and ink. Willie took a deep breath and wrote in his best hand a brief note to the old judge. After sending along his personal regrets at the judge's removal from office, Willie asked the all-important question. "Do you know anything about the disappearance of my father's will?" Willie wrote.

After finishing the letter, Willie handed it to Ellen. She nodded as she read. Then she folded the paper into an envelope and addressed it in her delicate hand.

"Travis will take it to the stage depot tomorrow," she said. "Sam Delamer just might find himself a little surprise."

Willie frowned as he saw a wicked smile spread across Ellen's face. He'd never seen that kind of hatred in her eyes before.

"Ellen dear," Mrs. Cobb called out then. "We'd best get that chicken cut up and start the frying."

"Duty calls," Ellen said, setting the letter on a small desk and heading to the kitchen. "Go visit some with Travis. It'll keep him from telling any of his war stories."

They shared a laugh. Then Ellen disappeared, and Willie walked outside to find his friend.

It wasn't hard for Willie to tell Travis was happy to be home. His old friend had a smile as big as Texas on that long face of his. But as they talked, Willie found that there was something filling the space between them.

"Sure, I'll ride down there and post that letter for you, Willie," Travis said. "But there's something you've got to promise to do for me."

"Anything I've got to give," Willie said.

"It's Ellen. She's got her mind all made up the two of you will hitch up and raise a dozen kids."

"I always figured that'd be how it would be," Willie said, surprised that it should even be questioned.

"You tell her so?"

"Never in so many words. But it's how I want it."

"You hold off saying it, Willie Delamer. There's trouble in this valley. I know Pa wouldn't like to be related to the cause of it. And I care too much for Ellen to see her come to grief."

"I'll have no part in bringing any sadness to her," Willie said. "On that you've got my solemn word. If you think it's best I not ask your father for his blessing till all this business about Sam and the fences is resolved, then you've got my word on it."

"You figure you can talk Sam out of what he's doing?" Travis asked.

"Nobody can talk Sam out of a thing," Willie said, kicking up a swirl of sand with his boot. "But if there's a will, then I don't see how he can keep me from what's mine. When I'm bound to fight, then I can be a man to be reckoned with."

"I know, Willie. But this man's your brother."

"I wonder," Willie said, staring at the blazing sun overhead. "We had the same mama and papa, but there's a difference in our hearts. He's out to mold the land, set it on a forge and hammer it out to his liking, stamp that trident brand of his on its rump like a longhorn steer. He even tore down the scaffolds on the cliffs, Trav. He means to change it all."

"Listen, Willie," Travis said, taking the hand of his friend and turning him toward the river. "Lots of men have come down to this valley and tried to tame it. You can break a horse by taking the spirit out of it or you can gentle it till it puts its proud head on your shoulder. Both horses'll run, but the first, he runs from fear. The second runs with his heart.

"Sam can break a horse by bending it to his will. That don't work on the land. You got to understand the land, feel the warmth in its soil. You got to feel the heat on your back and taste the sweat from your forehead."

"That's how it used to be," Willie said. "Now they got their Yank judge and all those laws. Troops of blue-shirted cavalry ride around to back it up. God, I wish Papa'd come back. He'd know what to do."

"He'd shoot one Sam Delamer," Travis said. "Or the sight of all those fences would break his heart."

Willie turned away and stared at the distant hills that marked the location of the river. He knew from the worried look on Travis Cobb's face that it wasn't Bill Delamer that was really being discussed at all.

"I'll get the letter to the judge if I have to hand it to the old man myself," Travis said, slapping Willie on the back. "You can count on me."

"I know that," Willie said. "I just wish I could say the same to you. If it was fighting Indians or Yanks, I'd know what to do. But this war's got to get itself fought in court with papers and books and such. And that Yank judge's set to be the winner."

After a fine supper of chicken and dumplings, Travis rode for the stage depot down on Bluff Creek. It was where the Overland Mail crossed the Brazos. Willie and Ellen walked out past Mrs. Cobb's garden and sat in the soft clover beside three live oaks.

"I've got a strong feeling for you, Willie," Ellen told him. "I thought before I might be a fool of a girl thinking about you all that time. It's more, though. Standing close to you, I know I need to belong to you."

"Yeah," Willie said, smiling. "I used to think I could ride through a hundred battles and be hard enough no bullet could scratch me. I used to figure a strong man didn't need anybody. But to live, a man needs more than that."

"He needs a wife," she said, leaning her soft cheek against his.

"I can't talk of that yet," Willie said, touching her silky hair with his fingers. "There's too much to get done first. I won't be taking you to no fine white house on the top of a hill, Ellen, but there'll be a place for us down in some draw along the river where our kids'll run through the river and raise Cain just like we did."

"Willie, if there's not a will, take me to Colorado. You say Mary's getting along fine there."

"I'll be raising my family right here, Ellen," he told her.

"My roots are in this valley. I was born here. You can't dig up a tall oak and try to plant it somewhere else."

"Sam's many things, but he's no fool. He'll buy you off with some acreage. Maybe the south bank of the bend. We could plant corn, make a life for ourselves."

"I don't know," Willie said. "You should've seen that map he's got. He wants it all. And he doesn't want me."

"Then be careful, Willie. Sometimes men go and disappear from this valley. Luke Granger. Ben Stephenson."

"They were good men," Willie said, standing up. "You mean they just up and vanished?"

"Nobody ever found a sign of them, but the Trident Ranch bought up their holdings for taxes."

Willie closed his eyes a minute. He saw the sword of the old one, the knight of Lyon. He remembered his father's promises to Yellow Shirt. He thought about the cliffs of the ancient ones, the promises he'd made to so many people.

"Ellen, I don't mean for our family to be cursed by every decent man and woman along the Brazos. Papa didn't intend it should be that way. I'm going to change some things."

Just then there was a commotion back at the house, and Willie led Ellen that way. Two brown horses stood at the hitching rack, lathered from a hard ride. A young man of sixteen or so stood screaming something at the house. A second man was trying to calm the first.

"What's going on?" Willie asked Ellen as they drew near.

"I don't know," Ellen said. "Lester's brought some news."

Something cold as ice ran down Willie's spine as he broke away from Ellen's hand and ran toward the house. Travis had ridden to the depot. He'd been carrying the letter to Judge Taylor. Something must have happened.

As Willie approached the house, the young man in front of him turned and stared hard into Willie's eyes.

"What's HE doing here?" the young man asked. "He's a Delamer!"

"He's a guest in my house," Mrs. Cobb said. "Your own brother's best friend."

"Pa?" young Lester asked, full of fire and hatred.

"He's got leave to be here," Art Cobb said, his voice sour and hesitant.

"You hear what I say, Pa?" Lester asked. "Them Delamers went and dammed the creeks. The Longs sold out this mornin', and Ike Raymond's like to follow. Can't grow no corn without water. Another month, we'll be fenced in."

"What do you know about this?" Mr. Cobb asked Willie. "You ride out here with your brother's terms?"

"No, sir," Willie said, hands on his hips. "I told you before, sir. Sam doesn't discuss his business with me. I know about his plans for the valley, but they're not mine. Where's his dam, Buffalo Creek?"

Art Cobb nodded, and Willie slapped his knee.

"There's ways a dam can get blown up," Willie said.

"Don't you go tellin' us how you're goin' out there to blow your brother's dam," Les Cobb said. "He's got ten men out there just waitin' for us."

"Then there'll be another way," Willie said, his heart pounding. "I won't see you forced off your land. You've my word on that."

"A Delamer's word belongs on a stable floor with the rest of the muck," Les said, spitting. "We got lots of your brother's word. 'Don't worry, Art, I got no interest in the south range. No hurry, Art. Them longhorns been runnin' free for years.' Well, old Sam's got the range and the cattle. Now he wants our farm."

"My name's not Sam," Willie said, standing clear of Ellen. "And my word's good as Colorado gold. When I say a thing, I mean to have it taken for the truth."

"Or what, big man?" Les asked, touching the trigger of the Colt revolver on his hip. "You think you can take me?"

"Stop that kind of talk, Les," Ellen said. "You don't even know this man."

"I know his name," Les said, spitting a second time. "And I know the world's a better place with one less of them!"

"Les!" Mrs. Cobb shouted, pulling two younger brothers back into the house.

"Boy, you're making a mistake," Willie said, the confusion draining from his eyes. "This isn't some game. A man can get himself killed real quick. I've seen it happen in a hundred places. And you'll find I don't need no ten guns like Sam does. One's more than enough."

"Willie?" Ellen asked, staring with disbelief at the terribly cold eyes that faced her brother.

"Well, Les, you make up your mind. If you think drawing that pistol's worth dying for, you go and do it."

A terrible silence fell over them all then. The rage which had filled Lester Cobb's face those past few minutes gave way to white terror. The boy could see death in the eyes of the man standing across from him. There was a heavy smell of sweat and leather, and in the background a sound of heavy breathing.

"Willie, that's my brother," Ellen said.

"He's as old as I was at Shiloh," Willie said. "Sometimes sixteen's old enough to be a man."

"Mostly it's a time to be confused," Ellen reminded him.

The words tore through Willie like a cyclone. Willie'd written that to her from a sickbed in Corinth after the battle.

"She's right, you know," Willie said at last. "And it's not right that anybody should die over words. Too many already have." He turned to Ellen's father, "I beg your pardon if I've caused any trouble for you or your family."

"Hold there!" Les yelled as Willie turned away. "It's not over."

"Then get it done!" Willie screamed, turning back to the young man with a violence in his eyes that froze them all.

Young Les drew his pistol in panic, and a single shot from Willie's Colt blew the gun from the youngster's hand. The boy clutched his bleeding fingers and pulled them to his side. A stunned Willie Delamer replaced his gun in its holster and turned back to Ellen.

"Travis said you'd bring trouble," she said, her eyes possessing a new coolness.

"I'm sorry," Willie said, his eyes closer to tears than at any time since his father's death.

"I think it's best you leave," Mr. Cobb said then, pointing to Willie's horse. "You're not welcome in this house."

"I'm sorry it had to be this way," Willie said. "It wasn't what I intended. I hope you'll explain to Trav that it wasn't my play. I hope you'll . . ."

"Get out of here!" Mr. Cobb yelled, shaking a shotgun at Willie. "Get out of here 'fore I fill your face with buckshot."

Willie walked to his horse and mounted it with a quickness that took him back to the days of riding in the cavalry. As he drew the horse away toward the gate, he turned back.

"I'll keep my promises, Ellen," he said. "And I'll do what I can about the dams."

Looking into her eyes, Willie thought he saw a spark of the old Ellen, the innocent girl he'd left behind in '61. He knew, though, that she'd seen a side of him he'd hoped to hide, and that could change things.

"Willie," she called to him then, the old affection making its return.

He thought to go to her, but Art Cobb pulled back the hammer of the shotgun, and he rode reluctantly on back to the Trident Ranch.

CHAPTER 9

Ψ

Willie rode away from the Cobb Ranch with a heavy heart. He couldn't help but remember the way the warmth in Ellen's eyes had faded when he'd drawn his pistol.

It's the hardness in me, Willie thought to himself. That hardness had gotten him through the war. Now it would keep him from the things he loved. He had to find a way to put aside the guns, the violence. He had to try and recapture the gentleness his mother had seen in him, the kindness his brother James remembered.

But could he? Willie wondered if it wouldn't take a hard and violent man to put an end to Sam Delamer's plans. Sam never listened to anyone who wasn't strong and firm. As boys Sam had often laughed about his brother Willie. Wild as an Indian, Sam had called him. The truth was that Sam hadn't even taken Willie into account.

Willie frowned as he realized Sam had changed the ranch, reshaped the valley with not the slightest concern for his brother. James would be sent to the city to learn the law.

63

Willie would just be left to ride the lonely fences of the south range.

In the days to follow, Willie learned all he could of his brother's operations, and one night while the watchmen were asleep, the dams on the creeks mysteriously blew up. It was too late for the Raymonds and the Longs, though. Bills of sale were already attached to the deeds on file in the Palo Pinto land office. But Willie'd kept his promise. The water flowed freely, even it if did flow mainly through Delamer land.

It did not go without notice. Sam kept a closer watch on his brother. Two days later Travis Cobb rode out to the line shack with news from Judge Taylor.

"The judge is coming out next week," Travis said. "And he's got a copy of the will, Willie. He wouldn't tell me everything, but the running of the ranch was left to you. That should change a thing or two."

"Does Sam know?" Willie asked.

"He won't get word till it's too late. The judge is already on his way. He sent Sam a telegram, but Les picked it up."

"How's his hand?" Willie asked.

"Stiff and sore," Travis said. "I should've warned you. Les has a hot temper. Lucky to still have his head, that boy."

"I can't tell you how sorry I am," Willie said, frowning. "And I fear Ellen won't forget it."

"Wrong on that account, Willie. She's asked to ride out here and see you herself, but Pa refused. Don't figure that'll stop her, though. You plan to ride this country the rest of the week?"

"Likely," Willie said, "Next week we start rounding up the strays. And there's the branding to get done."

"When do you figure Sam'll start the fencing?" Travis asked. "He can pinch us good if he wants, you know."

"I expect to have him busy on other things," Willie said, laughing. "Judge Taylor might have some hard news for him."

The two old friends shared a moment of bitter laughter. Then Travis nodded and rode away.

About the middle of that week Ellen Cobb rode out herself. No further news had come of Judge Taylor, but Willie was relieved to find the young woman more her old self.

"Sam sent riders out to tell Pa his terms of sale," Ellen said as they rode along. "Pa put two barrels of rock salt into their backsides."

"I'll talk to Sam," Willie said. "I'm sure doing no good by riding this country."

"Don't tell him about Judge Taylor," Ellen said. "And be careful."

"I will," he said, holding her hand for a long time. "Pay my respects to your family."

"I'm afraid they haven't changed much," she said. "Jess and Bobby mainly know you from Travis's stories, but Les only remembers being put in his place, and shot to boot. After Mr. Raymond pulled out, Pa's taken to shooting tin cans with Sam's name on them."

It was hard letting Ellen's soft hand slip away, but Willie knew it had to be done. They planned to meet in town when possible. Then Willie rode north, back toward the river and the headquarters of the Trident Ranch.

It was well toward sundown when Willie finally arrived at the big manor house. He turned over his horse to the stable hands, then walked inside the house, through the foyer and back to the room Sam used as his office. Willie didn't bother to knock, just opened the heavy oak door and stomped into the room.

Sam didn't take notice. He glanced up, smiled and told Willie to close the door.

"I thought you were riding the south boundary," Sam finally said.

"Which one?" Willie asked. "Seems you added some property since I went out there."

"Do from time to time," Sam said. "Might add some more. I've heard old Art Cobb wants to sell his place. Seems the climate out that way's turned hot."

"Oh?" Willie said, smiling to keep from exploding. "I heard he was sitting on his porch waiting to fill your men with holes if they came back out there."

"Well, that won't last long. In another week or so we'll have him fenced in. He won't be able to get to market, and that'll be the end of the Cobbs."

"No, I don't think you'd want to do that," Willie said. "If you were to try something like that, you might have trouble with those fences of yours, like you had with that dam at Buffalo Creek."

"The Cobbs do that?" Sam asked, growing more attentive.

"Let's just say a friend did it," Willie said, smiling.

"You?"

"Might be."

"Well, little brother, you might meet with an accident yourself if you keep sticking that nose of yours where it doesn't belong."

"That a threat, Sam?" Willie asked, moving around so that Sam could see the flash of anger in his eyes. "I don't much like threats."

"You take this for a truth, Willie Delamer," Sam said. "You go and interfere with my plans, there'll be another granite headstone on that little knoll. And it won't be for me."

"Now you hear me, Sam. Papa never intended you to run this ranch. I mean to have my say and more. You press me, I'll see to it you know some of the misery I've lived these last five years."

"Misery?" Sam said, laughing. "You revel in it. For Papa and you war is like a big game. You love to ride your chargers through the troops, listening to the shouts and the cheers. But men get killed leading their crusades, Willie."

"And most that lie and cheat get found out, Sam. People leave copies of things behind. Like wills."

Sam's face turned a bright shade of pink, and he slammed the books on his desk.

"Don't tread where you don't belong, Willie. You don't

fit around here now. I'd be happy to give you money, help you start a place of your own upriver. In Colorado, even."

"This is my home, Sam," Willie said. "And when I go, I'll be taking that sword there with me." Willie pointed to the bright weapon on the wall beside them. Sam frowned.

"My son will have that with him when he's elected governor," Sam said. "It's his birthright. As for you . . ."

"What did you do with the will, Sam?" Willie asked. "Burn it?"

"The only will Papa had was that the ranch should grow and prosper," Sam said. "And that's what it will do. James is young yet. He'll be provided for. As for you, it's about time you started earning your keep."

"What?" Willie asked, his eyes flashing fire.

"You heard me. You come in here thinking this whole place will be yours if you wish it so. Well, there isn't any will. You think you've done some big thing out there for the Cobbs, blowing up a dam. Well, all you did was cheapen the price they'll get for the land.

"They'll sell, just like all the others. As for you, you might be interested in some news I received. It seems a stage was involved in an accident out past Buffalo Draw. Two passengers were killed, one an old man who used to live near here. I don't believe they recovered any papers."

"Judge Taylor?" Willie asked.

Sam was silent.

"You had him killed," Willie said. "I wouldn't have believed you were capable of something like that."

"He died in the accident," Sam said. "If anyone was responsible for his death, you were. You brought him here. As for the will, Papa left none. If the judge had one, it was a forgery."

"You mean to steal it from me, don't you?"

"Steal? I never needed to, Willie," Sam said, laughing to himself. "You gave it up when you rode out of here with Papa. A ranch needs a builder. You never were. Now the Trident Ranch can grow, prosper."

"Prosper by sucking the blood from decent families Papa would have looked after."

"We'll prosper because of good management," Sam said. "We'll grow by building on the decaying foundations of little mud huts and log cabins of people who don't belong here."

"It's a sad thing, Sam."

"Is it?"

Willie left his brother alone in the office. An hour later Matthew carried the old war chest down and set it in the stable.

"Mr. Sam, he say you best earn your keep, sir," the black man said. "He say the stable need help."

"He does?" Willie asked, his face crimson.

"He say that to you, Mr. Willie," Matthew said, setting down the chest and retreating.

Willie thought to find Sam and have it out once and for all with him. But that wasn't the way to win, Willie thought. His father had taught him well. First you proved yourself, found some support. Then you went after the top dog. If you did that too soon, you only got yourself chopped up by the little pups.

Willie didn't take his place in the bunkhouse that night. Instead he took two blankets and rode out to the old cliff where the ancient scaffolds had once stood. He climbed the steep canyon wall with hesitation. It was a place that had once been full of peace, but there was no peace in Willie's heart. He expected to face as great a challenge in his brother as he had that fall when he'd shot his first buck, the spring when he'd ridden to war at his father's side.

It was dark when he reached the top of the cliff. The blackness of night clung to the place like a bridal veil. Willie sat for a time near where the old lances had stood. Then he stripped off his shirt and boots.

Memories of other times came flooding back through Willie's mind. He stepped to the edge of the cliff and dangled his toes over the side. The wind stirred, stinging his eyes and burning his bare chest. He closed his eyes and prayed.

"God, grant me the strength," Willie murmured as the wind grew fierce. "Help me do what has to be done."

A great flash of heat lightning lit the sky in front of him, and the ground shook. Willie felt a strange presence, something foreign and unearthly.

"I'm sorry I wasn't here to protect the old burial ground," Willie whispered. "I would never have let Sam desecrate the spirit cliffs."

The wind suddenly died, leaving the high ground echoing in an eerie silence. Then a wolf howled in the distance, and the spell was broken. Willie stepped back from the cliff and sat down, his legs crossed Indian fashion. As his eyes closed, a new calm came to his soul.

CHAPTER 10

Ψ

It was a different Willie Delamer that returned from the cliffs. He suddenly had his bearings. If the ranch was to be won back from Sam, it would have to be done through the force of his own personality. It was how his father had first captured the valley, by drawing the others to him.

It wasn't a new thing to Willie. Hadn't he risen in the ranks from private to major in a brief four years? Hadn't he been the one to earn the confidence of his men, the respect of his enemies? It could be done again.

Willie ignored Matthew's comments about the stable and rode instead to the east pasture. Most of the ranch hands were gathering there to begin the spring roundup, and he stood among them as the foreman of the ranch, a man named Franklin, began assigning men to the different stretches of range.

Before the war the broad flatlands around the Brazos had been open range. Over the years strays from different ranches had produced large herds of longhorns wandering across the land. The fencing of the Trident Ranch had brought those huge herds into Delamer hands.

Every spring the hands brought in all the stock for counting and branding. Gelding of bull calves would be done at the same time. Now the wild range cattle were brought in as well. All in all it promised to be a major undertaking.

Life as a cattleman was never easy, but roundup was more than just difficult. The men would be up before first light and work till dusk. It was dirty, back-breaking labor full of dust and sweat and blood. There was hardly a chance for eating and sleeping.

Willie'd never cared for roundup. It was the part of a ranch's operation which he liked least of all. He'd seen his first one at the age of ten. His father had taken him out to Crooked Tree Creek and turned him over to old Bob Hunt. Willie'd held down calves as Bob had done the gelding.

He could still remember the hissing sound of hot branding irons pressed into the hides of the animals. His ears rang with the squeals of calves as the cutting was done, and the foul smell of the buckets of blood and flesh as they putrified in the Texas heat nearly choked him.

Some of the men had laughed at Willie's white face. Most remembered their own first time and smiled. Others stared at the grim young face that refused to be sick or cry.

"Bill Delamer's boy," one remarked to another, nodding his head.

In the years that had followed Willie had done it all, branding, roping, gelding. His father had said it to him.

"Son, a man never asks another to do a thing he won't do himself. A strong man never was afraid to soil his hands in honest work."

Franklin chose no simple assignment for Willie. No branding or corral work was set before him. Instead the foreman pointed to six wild mustangs and handed Willie a rope.

"Break them horses," Franklin said. "We're short saddle mounts."

71

Willie glanced over at the horses, then paused. There was something familiar about Franklin's voice.

"You serve in the war, Franklin?" Willie asked.

"Two years," the foreman said.

"With Hood's Brigade maybe?" Willie asked, studying the man's face. "In Virginia?"

"Some," Franklin said. "That was a while back, though."

"I suppose," Willie said. "Still, I feel like I've seen you somewhere before."

"Well, could be," Franklin said. "'Course it seems to me every man with a limp or a scar looks like somebody."

"Maybe," Willie said. "It's more than that, though."

"No, don't see it could be," Franklin said. "I'd recalled the Delamer name when I came here. And you're the kind of man to be remembered. No, it's just I favor someone."

Franklin headed off to supervise the others, leaving Willie to his thoughts. The former major was fighting to take charge inside Willie's head, trying to remember where he'd seen or heard Franklin before. But there'd been so many faces, so many voices. Was Franklin some soldier who'd followed him into battle, some comrade who'd fallen at his side? Maybe Willie'd seen his face across a campfire on the frozen heights above Fredericksburg.

Willie shrugged it off. Franklin was right. All the faces looked familiar when you'd been in the army four years. Most men didn't see two or three hundred different faces in a lifetime. Willie must have seen thousands those last few years.

The mustangs stirred in the corral, and Willie shook away the remembering. There was a job to be done, and who Franklin was or whether they'd met before was unimportant.

Willie and a youngster named Brett Maxwell set to gentling the mustangs right away. Young Maxwell might have been seventeen, and Willie laughed at the boy's gangling legs and bony chest. He'd been around horses, though, and the two of them soon struck up a friendship.

Willie worked the horses in his own way, walking them and speaking softly. He tied sacks of grain to their backs

72

to get them used to the weight. At night Willie slept in the corral, letting the animals smell him, thus getting used to men.

That was all new to Brett Maxwell. The boy kept pointing to the other men working horses with whips and ropes.

"You can break a horse's spirit with a whip, Brett," Willie said, remembering his conversation with Travis Cobb, "but if you gentle him, touch his spirit with your own, you'll have the spirit under you when you need it. That horse'll race the wind."

"Touch its spirit?" Brett asked, shaking his head.

"The Comanches do it. Speak to the horse, let him know your smell. Get him feeling at ease with a man on his back."

"Talking to horses," Brett said, shaking his head. "My old grandpa told me there were some crazy mule-headed men working cows."

But while the others were laboring to bend the horses to their will, Willie had his six animals ready to be ridden in half the time. The other men soon gave more and more of their attention to Willie. They liked to listen to his stories of hunting buffalo with the Comanches. Some swapped stories of the Second Texas and Hood's Brigade. And the older ones, like Henry King, spoke of Big Bill Delamer and the war he fought against Yellow Shirt for control of the valley.

By the second week of roundup Willie knew most every hand by name. They'd watch him on a cutting horse, moving cows through the broken ground as if by magic. On horseback he was like a man with wings.

Only John Franklin, the foreman, seemed unimpressed. The others would have ridden to battle with Willie. Franklin gathered the men together one afternoon for a little corn liquor and some amusement. They did a little target shooting, some roping and racing, even rode a bull or two.

Willie sat on a fence post with Brett Maxwell and laughed with the others. All the men had worked hard, and it was rare to have time to relax. Then Franklin led out a tall black stallion and shouted a challenge to the crowd of ranch hands.

"Fifty dollars says there's not a man among you that can sit this horse!" the foreman yelled.

The men shouted back, jumping into the corral in turn to take their chance. The black horse reared and bolted, though, and it was all anyone could do just to catch him. Only two men got mounted, and they were thrown in a matter of minutes.

"Devil of a horse," Brett whispered to Willie. "Bet no man'll sit him all day."

Willie stared at the young man beside him. He could tell Brett was about to jump into the corral himself.

"No point to getting yourself maimed, Brett," Willie said. "Horse like that's got a hate for men. Look to his back and flanks. Spur scars and lash marks. Some men made that horse mean."

The others overheard. One of them, a tall man named Blane, suggested Willie take a turn.

"Come on, Major," another said. "Show him what a man is."

"What d'you say, Delamer?" Franklin asked. "Tell you what. I'll make it a hundred in gold. You stay on him two minutes, and the prize is all yours."

The crowd hooted and hollered, encouraged by the spirits and their fatigue. Willie looked at the younger men, those like Brett whose respect was needed to do what he planned. Willie stripped off his vest and handed it and his hat to Brett. Then he jumped into the corral and walked to the horse's side.

The others started to throw ropes over the horse's head, but Willie waved them off. Speaking softly some Spanish words learned years before in a Comanche camp, Willie approached the horse and touched its side.

"Get on him, Major!" someone shouted, and the horse grew nervous.

"Easy, big black," Willie whispered, touching its side again. "Touch my soul."

The horse whinnied and shied away, but Willie followed. Still the words were uttered. The crowd behind grew rest-

74

less, and some began slamming their hands against the fence posts. Willie ignored them, stroking the horse's nose and talking more.

"I'll be a polecat," one of the hands said as Willie slid onto the horse's back and clung to its neck as the horse began prancing around the corral.

"You already smell like one," someone said, and the crowd began laughing.

Franklin wasn't laughing at all, though. The foreman picked up a pebble and hurled it against the rear of the horse. Men shouted and frowned as the horse reared into the air and tried to dislodge the rider. Willie hung on, though, squeezing his strong arms around the animal's neck as he talked in a calming voice.

The horse was upset, though. It bucked and reared, then raced across the corral, banging its side against the fence so that Willie had to draw his right leg up to avoid being smashed. But as the animal struggled, the power in Willie's arms seemed to drain its spirit. Soon the creature relented, and Willie sat up on the animal's back, proudly listening to the yells of the other men.

When he dismounted, Willie waited a moment for Brett to bring his hat and vest. Then Franklin handed the former major the five promised twenty-dollar gold pieces.

"Three cheers for the major!" somebody shouted.

The cheers rang through the valley for ten miles.

The last of the cattle were rounded up that afternoon, and Sam rode out toward nightfall to select the steers that would be driven to Fort Belknap for the army. James came along in the carriage, and Willie found himself alone with his younger brother as the sun settled into the western sky.

"How come you came out here?" James asked. "Sam send you?"

"Partly," Willie said. "Sam stole the ranch, you know. Papa left it to all of us in his will. I should be running the place."

"I know all about the will," James said, surprising Willie not a little.

"You what?"

"Look, Willie, that will doesn't mean anything. Judge Fulton would use it to break up the ranch, take over the valley for himself. The only way to fight the Yanks is to have one strong ranch, one man in charge."

"You've changed a lot, Jamie," Willie said, using the name he'd called his brother as a boy.

"I told you before, Willie, I've outgrown the stories."

"And what about right and wrong? Do you go along with what Sam's done to the others?"

"Judge Fulton won't always be around, Willie," James said. "Then it will be our turn. For now, you just go along with Sam and he will probably turn over half the operation to you."

"There was a time when the Delamers stood for something," Willie said. "You don't remember Papa, but he came here to build a better place, not just a bigger one."

"I remember Papa," James said, his face grim and solemn. "But when Papa died, you were gone. I stayed with Mary for a time, but since then Sam's been all the family I've had. I know he's a hard man, but he's family, Willie. We all are."

"I don't mean to hang him, James."

"Then what?"

"I want him to turn over the ranch operations to me. There'll still be money, lots of it. But the people of the valley are being run off, and that's not right. It has to stop."

"You haven't been here long, Willie. It's better for us to be taking this land than for the Yanks to be stealing it for taxes."

"James, there isn't any other way for me. I don't know anybody else to be."

"Then be careful, Willie. Sam's not an easy man to beat."

"Neither am I," Willie said, smiling at his younger brother. Willie got less conversation from Sam. The older Delamer stared long and hard at the younger, and it was clear no love was shared between the two of them.

"Hear you found your place with the horses," Sam finally said.

"Horses make better company than some men," Willie said through his teeth.

"Got some work for you boys tomorrow that you'll really take to, Willie," Sam said. "Fences."

There was a terrible look of contempt on Sam's face then, and it was all Willie could do to restrain the rage that raced through his body.

"There'll be more words between us, Sam," Willie said. "And before too long, I expect."

"I don't think there's anything that hasn't already been said," Sam said. "Unless you'd like some traveling money."

As the carriage carrying his brothers disappeared into the darkness, Willie spit in the ruts its wheels left. Then he walked away to find a place to spread his blankets, a place away from the others where he might feel close to the night sky.

CHAPTER 11

Ψ

The next morning Willie rode westward with Franklin and Brett Maxwell. Most of the men had gone south to move the line of frences down to include the Long and Raymond farms. Willie couldn't stand the thought of it. The Cobb place would be cut off just like old Art Cobb had said.

For a time he thought to go along, disrupt the work, cut the wire. But that would do little except anger the hands. Travis could take care of opening the market roads, and it wouldn't be long before Willie was ready to make his move for control of the ranch. Then all that fence would be torn down.

Building fences along the western boundary of the ranch was not a job taken lightly. Rugged hills filled most of that country, and for years they alone had served to keep the cattle on Delamer lands. With so many cattle now, though, Sam had decided to enclose the whole ranch with wire.

For a man like Willie who hated fences to find himself working so hard to put them up was one of those ironies fate seemed to deal Willie. The ground was rocky, and it fought the post hole digger every inch of the way.

As the digger scraped the flaky limestone, terrible whines filled the air. The blades were pounded, and no deep holes could be dug. But the posts were set in place nonetheless.

The job wasn't made any easier by the midafternoon sun. With sweat soaking his shirt and dripping from his forehead, Willie began wishing he was back in Virginia. He remembered the cool breezes of the Shenandoah Valley with fondness. But the heat was part of being home, and he wiped his forehead and went on with the work.

As Willie dug the holes, Brett and Franklin cut down scraggly mesquite trees and readied the wire. When ten holes were dug, the three of them would work together to sink the posts and string the wire.

Franklin would carefully roll the strands of wire from the wide rolls in the wagon. Brett would then hold it in place as Willie nailed it to the posts. If the tension was not maintained just right, the wire would fly up and become tangled.

The three men worked swiftly, but carefully. Young Brett Maxwell had steady hands, and Willie rarely missed the nails. Franklin was used to the wire after three years as foreman at the Trident, and the posts were held firmly.

After taking a break from building fences to eat some beef jerky, they started back to work. Willie was soaked with sweat, and only his leathery skin kept him from being sunburned. He took off his shirt and wrung it out. His muscular arms and shoulders dripped with perspiration so that the scars appeared more pronounced. He could feel Brett's eyes on the jagged mark made long before by a Comanche lance. The scars made Franklin nervous. Willie noticed the foreman bore none of his own.

As the unrelenting heat of the afternoon drained them of their energy, Franklin finally cut the wire and announced they'd done enough for one day. Leaving the wagon and horses beside the fence, the three men walked a few hundred yards to a small creek. There they dove into the chill waters and tried to cool off.

The water washed away the dirt and sweat. More than that it cast from Willie the weariness of the day's labor. He felt young and strong again. Hard work had been a way of life for as long as he could remember. As he sat in the water and relaxed, he noticed a movement in the thicket beyond the creek.

Willie said nothing. He motioned for the others to be quiet, then rolled out of the water and crawled to where he'd put his revolver. Shielding himself behind a tall mesquite, Willie drew his gun and searched for an intruder.

He could hear the heavy breathing of Brett Maxwell behind him, could hear the heavier footsteps of Franklin farther back.

"Over there," Brett whispered, pointing to a clearing maybe two hundred yards to the left.

"Comanches," Willie said.

Brett took his rifle and prepared to fire, but Willie pushed the gun away.

"They've got some of our beef, Willie," the young man said, pointing. "Look, three cows."

"Look at them," Willie said, waving at the nearest Indian. "Near starving. Only four altogether, and two look to be younger'n you are. I wouldn't shoot a man over three cows, especially if he was starving."

"What is it?" Franklin asked, joining them.

"Indians," Brett said. "Four of them. Painted for war, too."

Willie hadn't noticed that before. Sure enough the men had dabbed bright red and yellow paint on their faces and bare chests. Only one carried a rifle, though. They were hardly a threat.

"We can take 'em, Delamer," Franklin said. "You take the two in the middle. Maxwell the left, me the right."

"Don't be a fool," Willie said. "Killing them wouldn't help us, and there might be more around."

"You just mean to leave 'em be?" Franklin said.

"I figure it'd be best if we got word to the others. We're near half a day's ride from the house, and more than that from the men down south."

"I count fourteen men along this section," Franklin said. "Maxwell, you ride down Buffalo Creek and fetch the others. Send somebody to the big house with word."

"And tell the Cobbs," Willie said. "They'll help."

Franklin seemed surprised. The foreman thought to say something, then stopped. There was gunfire in the distance, and the Indians raced off with their cattle, whooping and shouting like madmen.

"Spencer's bunch," Franklin said. "Other side of the hollow."

"We'd best get over there," Willie said. "Leave the wire?"

"I sure don't plan on draggin' it along. Let's go!"

The two men rode through the creek and over two low hills. Smoke hung in the air in a low area, and they headed that way. A line of new fence stopped fifty feet short of a small cluster of juniper trees. There lay three bodies, still and lifeless.

"Spencer?" Franklin called, gasping for air.

Willie left the foreman frozen on his horse and moved to the dead men. Drawing the rifle from behind him, Willie slid down off Thunder and walked forward. The unmistakable sounds of Comanches filled the air not fifty yards in front of them.

The men hadn't been dead long. Blood still flowed from some of the wounds, and the smell of death was not yet strong. Dark masses of flies scattered as Willie came near. It wasn't a pretty sight.

The three men had all been shot with rifles. Spencer also had a slash down his forehead which had closed one eye, probably made by a war ax. Dark patches of red marked the foreheads of each man. They'd been scalped.

Franklin had gotten down from his horse. The foreman vomited in the high grass behind the farthest corpse, that of a man Willie hardly knew. The men's guns were gone, as were their horses. Articles of clothing, watches and a few other trinkets had also been taken.

Willie walked past the bodies and examined the ground. Many unshod ponies left their tracks. Bloodstains could be found in the grass. The ranch hands had hit someone.

"How many?" Franklin asked, still gasping for air.

"Twenty maybe," Willie said, looking over the ground. "What you've got here is a band of them come back."

"Come back?" Franklin asked. "Back to what?"

"Home," Willie said. "They've likely got a village up the river a ways."

"Village for who?" Franklin asked.

"What do you mean?" Willie asked. "For their women and little ones, of course."

"Not unless they done a lot of fancy trading," Franklin said. "We rode down most of 'em four summers back. Cut 'em down one and all."

"Children?" Willie asked.

"Everybody," Franklin said. "There were men who had their pleasure with the squaws first. But in the end we shot 'em all."

"My God," Willie said, his eyes dying. "Did Sam know?"

"Know?" Franklin asked. "He led us!"

Willie walked out into the trees and leaned on a mesquite. Thorns from a branch pricked the skin of his bare shoulder, but he failed to notice. So Sam had ridden down women and children? Now the men had finally come back. There would be no treating with such warriors. Their lives were over. Only death would follow.

As Willie fought to control his anger, he heard a movement to his right. He turned to face a tall warrior holding a war lance. As Franklin raised his gun, a rifle shot toppled the foreman. Willie's fingers touched his pistol, but his eyes met the Indian's.

"You are Gray Swallow," Willie said, recognizing the man's face. "You hunted with Red Wolf and me before the war against the blues shirts."

Recognition came to the Indian's eyes, and the man frowned.

"Go and tell Red Wolf I would speak with him," Willie said. "Tell him you have seen the scar which still marks my bow arm."

The Indian rode forward and touched the point of his lance to Willie's shoulder.

"If you would take my life, do it," Willie said, his eyes hard and cold. "But tell my brother Red Wolf of it. Say to him that I killed no Comanche."

The face of the Indian grew tense. Three others joined the man, and they prepared to finish off Franklin.

"Leave him," Willie said with a voice that roared like thunder through the trees. "Go to Red Wolf and tell him what I said. Say to him that I wait for him here."

Gray Swallow said nothing. But when he turned his horse and motioned for the others to follow, it was clear that Willie'd made himself understood.

Willie walked to where Franklin lay, blood oozing from a great hole in his chest.

"Can you walk?" Willie asked.

"I think so," the foreman said, staggering to his feet.

Willie tore a strip from Spencer's shirt and bound the foreman's wound. The two men then made their way to a shaded area overlooking the woods.

As they sat together, Willie found himself staring at the man beside him. Something strange ran through his brain. It was as if he was doing something he'd done before. The sound of cannons echoed through his memory, and the smell of gunpowder in the air grew stronger.

"You remember, don't you?" Franklin asked.

"Gettysburg," Willie said. "Devil's Den. I brought you water."

"You thought I was gut shot," Franklin said, moaning. "It was only blood, though."

"You ran," Willie said, his eyes harsh just then. "All those boys dead and dying, and you ran."

"Lots of us did," Franklin said. "We were scared."

83

"There's no running now."

"Them Comanches'll be back, won't they?"

"You can count on that," Willie told Franklin.

"You figure I'll last that long?"

"Maybe," Willie said, feeling his anger fade a little.

"Good," the man said. "I'd like to go out with a rifle in my hands. Not like Gettysburg."

They sat in silence for a time. Then Franklin sat up and coughed.

"Got something to say to you, Delamer," Franklin said.

"There'll be time later," Willie said.

"Got to be now," the foreman said. "Might not get a chance when them Indians get here."

"Go on then," Willie said.

"Your brother," Franklin said, coughing again. "He paid me to . . . to get you out of the way."

"What?" Willie asked.

"He sent for . . ."

Before Franklin could finish, his eyes became glassy, and blood trickled from his lips. Willie recognized the signs of a man shot through the lungs. Before anything else could be said, Franklin's chest stopped its labored movements, and a heavy smell hung in the air. Willie closed the man's eyes and picked up his rifle.

As Willie walked away, he found himself trying to recall the man's real name. It would be good to put it on his marker. But he realized others would want to know the story, and the man would be best remembered as Franklin in the Brazos Valley, no matter what was written on his tombstone.

Willie sat a long time under a broad live oak, smelling the wild onions all around him, listening to a cardinal singing in the branches overhead. Then the birds scattered, and the air grew silent. Out of the woods in front of him rode a broad-chested Comanche in his twenties, a hard stare painted on a solemn face.

Willie recognized the Indian immediately in spite of the years that had separated them. As the man drew his horse to a halt, Willie cradled the rifle in his arms and walked forward. The two men faced each other in silence for several minutes. Then Red Wolf frowned and spat on the ground near Willie's feet.

"You would speak to me?" the Comanche finally asked.

"If you have ears for my words," Willie said.

"A dead man has ears for no man's words," Red Wolf said, tearing open his shirt so that Willie could see the death sign painted there.

"Then I would sit with you for a time, old friend," Willie said. "Perhaps it is a good day to die."

The two of them stared hard at each other. No smile crossed either man's cracked lips. Tension stiffened their shoulders, and anger swept their hearts. There was a feeling of violence in the air, and even the lizards stopped their scurrying.

The two old friends stood frozen for what seemed an eternity. Willie faced Red Wolf alone, his back to the four dead ranch hands. Red Wolf sat upon his tall white horse. Thirty Comanches stood behind him, painted and ready for war.

In another time Willie would have been welcomed to the camp of Red Wolf and the Comanches. There had been a time when he had been. But the men he faced now had painted the mask of death on their chests. There was no thought of living, only killing their enemies on the hated Trident Ranch and then finding what peace death could offer.

Willie finally held his rifle out with his hands and spat on the ground in front of the young chief.

"I have no hatred for the Comanche," Willie said, casting the rifle into the high grass to his left. He then slung his pistol and knife in the same direction.

"Red Wolf, our blood has stained the same knife, has flowed within each other's veins. Long ago my life was given up into your hands. If you would take it now, then do it."

Willie stepped back and pounded his chest.

"You have marked my flesh twice, Red Wolf. Once on the bow arm," Willie said, pointing to the scar, "and once on the wrist," he added, showing the mark made by the knife which had bound them together as brothers. "Do you wish to mark it again?"

Willie tried to cast the coldness from his eyes, tried to recapture the peace he'd found on the cliffs.

"I will hear your words, Bright Star," Red Wolf said at last, using the name given Willie so long ago when the two men had chased each other across the land as boys.

Red Wolf waved the other Comanches away, then jumped from his horse and led the way to a rocky place shaded by tall oak trees. The two men sat across from each other, folding their arms and bending their legs beneath them.

"You have been gone for many summers," Red Wolf finally said. "The earth has changed."

"I know," Willie said. "Even the spirit cliffs no longer stand as they did."

A terrible look of pain came to Red Wolf's eyes, and the Comanche slammed his fist down hard on the ground.

"This was not my doing," the Indian said.

"But you cut the Treaty Oak. How can that be?" Willie asked.

"It was not the Comanche who broke the treaty," Red Wolf said angrily. "It was not at the hand of the Comanche that Yellow Shirt, my father, found his death."

"Tell me about it," Willie said. "I want to know."

"It is a thing of great pain for me, Bright Star. I am the last of my father's sons, and his spirit does not rest lightly upon me. My father had a dream. The spirits spoke to him, saying that when Tall Star, your father, left this place, the earth would be no more."

Willie nodded his head sadly. He remembered the story of how the Comanches had named his father. The star had come from the flag of the Republic of Texas. It was a name of respect.

"Yellow Shirt rode to stop your father," Red Wolf said. "But it was dark, and many white men had come to the valley. One such had no eyes to see the peace in my father's heart. A gun was fired, and the eyes of Yellow Shirt saw no more light.

"There were those in the camp of the Comanche who spoke for peace. But there was no peace. Whites shot many of our men, and some took children to work as slaves. We mourned for Yellow Shirt. Then we painted our faces and rode to battle."

"Battle? You burned our house, killed a boy not two years old! Is this how the Comanche makes war?"

"No, this is the war brought by your brother to us," Red Wolf said. "He brought fire to the place of the ancient ones. He scattered the bones of my father in the river. He rides from warriors, but he raids our village. If I kill little ones, it is because they are in battle. This son of your own father comes to my camp, kills the young men who fight. Then he takes others, women and children.

"Comanche takes captive, makes slave. This dark one burns lodges, then kills all. He even kills those who do not yet walk. The cry of the dead screams out for this man's death. Only his dying will bring peace to the spirits of the dead."

Red Wolf shook with emotion, and Willie bit down on his lip to keep from crying out. Sam had done that? He'd murdered children? Shot them down after the village was taken?

"My heart is sad for your people," Willie said. "These things make this man no brother to me. I do not take to his lodge, nor will I take his hand in mine."

"Your heart is good, Bright Star, but it matters little. Your voice is not a great one in the camps of the whites. We have painted the mark of death on our chests. Soon the earth will know the voice of the Comanche no longer."

"It doesn't have to be that way," Willie said. "You can have the lands where your village once stood. I will see to it that such is done."

"You would have it so, my brother, but this cannot be. There is too much anger in the heart of the dark one. And what life waits for the Comanche? To grow old without the touch of a woman? To never hear the songs of the little ones? Such is no life."

"And is there nothing I can do?"

"Remember the summers you passed in the camps of Yellow Shirt. Remember the buffalo moon, the time of the deer hunt. Do not forget the power of the spirit cliff. You may have need of it if the earth would not be sold to the dark ones."

"And you?"

"I will ride through the earth like a fire on the prairie wind. Much will burn, and many will die. There will be no tomorrows for Red Wolf."

"I will mourn your passing, my friend," Willie said. "And I will long remember."

"Guard your spirit, Bright Star," Red Wolf said solemnly. "There is a darkness in your soul which grows. It is better to lose the earth than to lose your spirit."

"Is it possible to keep your spirit and lose the earth?" Willie asked, his piercing blue eyes searching those of his friend for the answer they both knew.

"I leave you now," Red Wolf said, standing. "I fear I will not speak to you again as a man."

Willie looked deeply into the sadness written on the Comanche's face. If they met again it would be as enemies. It was a thing they both had feared. And now it had come to pass.

Red Wolf mounted his horse and rode away. Willie picked up his guns and headed for the wagon. He brought it to the hollow, then piled the four bodies in the back. The horses were tied to the rear. Then Willie headed south in search of the others.

CHAPTER 12

Ψ

Willie finally drove the wagon into the camp of the other ranch hands shortly before nightfall. The wonderful aroma of boiled potatoes and barbecued beef filled the air. Willie might have felt hungry, but the stench coming from the back of the wagon was too overpowering.

Willie stumbled off the wagon and walked forward to the other men. Most were laughing and eating. But there were few smiles after Willie staggered into their midst.

"Franklin's dead," Willie announced, catching his breath.

"What?" Henry King gasped.

"Indians. Thirty or so," Willie told them. "Be here by dawn."

The faces around him turned white. Some reached instinctively for their guns.

"Young Maxwell rode through to tell all about the Comanches," Henry said. "Then he left to tell the others."

"Isn't he back?" Willie asked.

"He only got out here an hour or so," one of the men said. "It'll take most of the night to reach the south range."

"Who's gone to the house?" Willie asked.

The others exchanged nervous looks. They turned back to Willie and shook their heads.

"No one I know of," Henry said.

Willie glanced along the line of men. Altogether there were but nine of them. When he came to a slim young man about eighteen, he sighed.

"Send him," Willie said, pointing to the young man.

"Don, you know the road to the big house," Henry told the young man. "You get down there and tell Sam Delamer there's a party of Comanches out here. Tell him to get word to them Yank troopers. And if there's help to be had, you have him send it."

Young Don walked to the horses and drew his mount away. In a matter of minutes the boy had the animal saddled. Willie smiled as the lone rider headed east down a winding road.

"You know there won't be any help to get this far 'fore morning," Henry said. "And I never yet seen eight men hold off any Comanche war party."

"I know," Willie said. "But if we hold up, form a tight perimeter and fight hard, we might last till help gets here."

"Easy for you to say with that Spencer's rifle," one of the men said. "But we mostly got pistols and old Harpers Ferry rifled muskets. Ain't much use in no Indian war."

"Maybe not," Willie said. "But you might pick off a man or two that way, and your pistol's good for close in fighting. There's high ground close by full of boulders and mesquites, with a spring for water. We can move on up there tonight."

The men looked around, nodding. There was a murmur of agreement, and confidence seemed to surface in their eyes.

"You tell us how to fight it, Major," a tall man dressed in dark black said. "I fought at Elkhorn Tavern, and Jennings over there was at Vicksburg."

A smaller man nodded. Willie recognized two of the others from the old Second Texas that had fought at Shiloh. He felt better knowing there were veterans around him.

The men moved to the high ground after nightfall, leaving a false campfire to deceive the Indians. The horses were made secure in a picket line, and positions were prepared for defending the hill. Sentries were posted throughout the night, but no sign of Comanches or help came.

When morning came, Willie got the men into position and readied them for the attack that was bound to come. Before breakfast was fully cooked, the earth shook with the pounding of hooves. Soon Red Wolf rode into a clearing below. Behind him were thirty warriors, all painted with the mask of death.

"They've got some strange kind of black paint on their chests and faces," Henry said to Willie. "Never seen it before."

"It means they're going to die today," Willie said. "Red Wolf told me yesterday. I don't think any of them care whether they live or not."

"But they mean to kill a few of us, huh?"

"More than likely they will," Willie said. "Let's dig in."

As the ranch hands loaded and aimed their weapons, there was a sudden movement through the ranks of the Indians. The men on the hill mumbled.

"Lord, it's young Don Keller," Henry said.

Willie stared as the Comanches drew out the boy who'd gone for help. Blood trickled down his bare chest from dozens of cuts. His hands were tied behind him, but Willie knew there were cuts in the boy's hands as well. Comanches sometimes sliced off whole fingers and toes. Thinking about it turned Willie's stomach.

The Indians surrounding they boy hooted and screamed. Willie swallowed and looked into the young man's eyes. They were bloodshot from lack of sleep and white with fear. But the Comanches dragged him from his horse and shouted for him to run.

The men on the hill yelled their encouragement. Don was tired and weak from loss of blood, but it was clear the boy was running for his life. And run he did, hard and swift as a deer. Pain flashed across his face as he took each step.

The strain in his chest, the ache in his legs showed a determination to survive. But as he neared the crest of the hill, Willie heard a terrible laugh arise from the Comanches. A shot rang out, and the boy fell dead before their eyes.

"Blamed Comanches," Henry said, standing up. "Come on, you devils!"

It was what the Comanches wanted. Another shot rang out, and old Henry, the veteran of San Jacinto, fell stone dead at Willie's side. Then the valley exploded with gunfire. Arrows filled the air. Wild whoops shattered the stillness of the morning, and warriors raced up the hill on horseback.

Willie shouted to the others. Muskets and pistols barked out their answers, and riders toppled off their ponies. Two of the hands cried out as they were struck down by war lances. Willie shot two young warriors, and dodging a lance, killed a third.

Another Comanche fell from the saddle, taking an enemy with him. Two more ranch hands were cut off and run through with lances. Willie found himself and the other surviving white man turn to face the remaining Comanches. As the Indians prepared a final charge, Willie reloaded his rifle and made sure of his aim.

I never imagined it would end like this, Willie thought to himself. And not at the hands of Red Wolf.

There was no time to think of anything else. A terrible cry split the air below them, and Indians swarmed up the hill.

Willie never noticed when the man beside him was shot down. He didn't see how many Indians fell around him as he sprayed the air with bullets. He fought hand to hand with one enemy as another stood ready to finish him. Then he heard the sound of horses below, and shouts drew the attention of the Comanches.

Willie's knife found the first Comanche's chest, gashing deep enough that the life flowed from the man. A pistol shot killed the other. Willie's eyes were on fire as he stood alone on the hilltop and watched a wild skirmish take place below as the long-awaited relief arrived.

Willie stared at Red Wolf, his eyes frozen to the face of his old friend. The Indian sat on the tall white horse and chanted to the sky. One by one the other Indians fell. Then finally a bullet blew a great hole in his chest, and the last son of Yellow Shirt fell dead.

The rest of the fight passed quickly. Wounded Comanches were finished off without mercy. A few death chants still filled the air, but they were soon quieted. Brett Maxwell and Travis Cobb rode to the crest of the hill and shouted with relief when they found Willie. Willie himself walked sadly past his friends and looked at the carnage on the hill. Old Henry King, blood still dripping from where a Comanche had taken his scalp, lay stiff, his eyes staring blankly at the sky. Young Don Keller, the fingers of his left hand missing, was crumpled over a rock.

Some of the others shed tears for friends and relatives among the dead. Some prayed. Some began the burying, and there were those who stripped the bodies of the Indians of trinkets that would serve as mementos.

Willie stumbled past Travis and Brett on down the hill to Red Wolf. The man's face was already pale with death, and his body had been stripped of the great war bonnet and silver bracelets. His bow was gone, as were his painted leggings and shield.

"Willie?" Travis called out as Willie picked up the body of the dead Comanche.

"He was a friend," Willie said. "Leave me to myself just now."

"You're wounded," Brett said, pointing to a knife wound in Willie's arm.

"It'll heal," Willie said. "I'll meet you back at the house."

"And the rest of us?" one of the men asked. "There's still work to be done."

"No, we've done enough fencing," Willie said, giving Travis a strange glance. "Especially along the south range."

"Willie?" Brett said, frowning.

"Send 'em all back to the house, Brett," Willie said. "There's been enough fighting in this valley for one day."

"Whatever you say," the boy answered, walking toward the others.

Most of the men rode straight for the big house. The Cobbs and some of the others who had homes to the south went there. Willie tied the body of Red Wolf across the tall white horse, then mounted Thunder. He then headed east to the place they'd gone together before, when the valley had known peace, when there'd been time to hunt and grow tall in the way it was intended to be.

Willie'd never seen an Indian buried in the ground. All of the Comanches were placed on scaffolds in high places like the ancient ones. The old burial ground had been erased, but the cliffs were still there. And it was to that place that Willie took the body of his old friend Red Wolf.

It was no small task carrying the Indian's stiff body up the steep path to the top of the cliff. More than once Willie's legs buckled under the burden. But finally he stood atop the cliff, staring out across the valley that seemed stained by blood.

It would have been no great challenge to build a wooden scaffold from the tough old mesquite trees that grew on the summit of the cliffs. Willie dragged his friend's body to a ledge where the body of a great chief of the ancient ones had once rested. It was a sacred place, and he felt uneasy walking there.

A ritual should have been performed before the grave was made ready, but Willie knew nothing of the ceremony. He spread a blanket out on the ledge, then tore his shirt apart. He soaked the cloth in the water of a small spring and began washing the blood and dirt from the dead Comanche.

It was a long and unpleasant task. The flesh was rigid, and flies had gathered. When the washing was finally completed, Willie set the body on the blanket and replaced the painted breechclout that was the only scrap of clothing Willie had saved from the scavengers.

As Willie sat beside the ledge, dirt and bloody, the wind stirred in a strange way. Clouds moved in and covered the stars. Thunder shook the earth, and lightning flashed across the heavens. A brief downpour wet Willie's bare shoulders and brought a chill to his soul.

Then, as suddenly as it had come, the rain vanished, leaving a bright sky overhead. Willie leaned his weary head against the cold wall of the cliff and remembered two boys running naked through the Brazos years before.

"The earth has changed, Red Wolf," Willie said softly. "Tomorrow I must return to the living."

As Willie lay back and closed his eyes, the spirits of the cliff seemed to whisper something to his soul. Not words exactly. It was more of a feeling, a warning. Somehow he knew facing Sam would be far from the simple thing he'd imagined. And he couldn't ignore the words of Franklin, either. There was someone to be watched for.

CHAPTER 13

Ψ

Sam Delamer paced the floor of the room anxiously. On his desk lay two letters, one from Judge Fulton and the other from the military commander at Fort Belknap.

"Can't trust anybody," Sam said, grumbling.

Since he'd taken control of the ranch, there'd never been a time like this. Just as he was about to finish off the last of those stubborn old farmers, Art Cobb, Willie had to come back.

It should have been a simple thing to deal with his brother. James had been handled so easily it hadn't occurred to Sam that Willie might be a problem, especially after he shot that fool Winthrop. But there'd been the dam on Buffalo Creek and now this business with Red Wolf's Comanches. The hands looked to Willie like some sort of magician with a rifle. There could be no thought of just sending him away now.

"I underestimated him," Sam said, kicking the side of the desk. "He's just like Big Bill. But he's got weaknesses, and I don't."

96

There were more immediate problems to be faced. The Indian raid had left the Trident short of men. And there were few extra hands to be found in the valley. Even boys of twelve were working from dawn to dusk.

Plans would have to be put off. After the Cobbs came out to rescue Willie and the fence crews, none of the men would touch a string of wire on the southern boundary. There was no one to do the work anyway. Just tending the cattle would be more than enough for the men to manage.

The other thing had to be taken into consideration, too. He reached over and took the two letters into his hand. The judge had just created a tax on cattle. The other letter stated that the army would not honor its contracts for cattle.

A coincidence? Sam doubted it. After going along with Sam's moves against the farms and other ranches of the valley, the carpetbagger had finally turned his attention to the Trident. This new tax would drain the cash reserves, and without revenue from beef sales to the army, the land tax would be impossible to pay. No one in the valley would buy land, and it was all Sam had to sell. The ranch would go for taxes, and there was little doubt as to who would buy it.

Sam tossed the letters angrily on his desk and wiped sweat from his forehead. The house was always warm in the spring, but the sweat wasn't the result of heat. A tremor of panic was surfacing inside Sam, and for the first time he was beginning to doubt his ability to save the ranch.

In accumulating the vast acreage Sam had been ruthless. He'd turned on friends and enemies alike. He was feared throughout the valley. Such men, even if they were to ask for help, seldom received it. As always Sam Delamer found himself alone.

The telegram he'd written the night before lay beside the discarded letters on his desk. He took it in his fingers and read it a final time.

JOHNSON. NEED YOUR SERVICES. S. DELAMER. TRIDENT RANCH.

With reluctance Sam crumpled the telegram in his hand

and hurled it against the wall. It bounced back to his foot, and he kicked it into a corner of the room.

"Papa?" said a small voice from the doorway.

Sam turned and opened the door, angry at being disturbed when so much was on his mind.

"Papa, Uncle Willie's back," spoke young Robert Delamer, hiding his frail six-year-old body behind the door for protection from the rage on his father's face.

"A gentleman knocks on a closed door, Robert," Sam said, regaining his composure. "Tell Matthew I'll see Willie in a moment.

"He's all bloody," Robert said. "Somebody tore his shirt, and there's blood all over his arm."

The boy was obviously shaken, and another man might have tried to comfort him. Sam just smiled.

"If you hope to manage this ranch one day, Robert, you'll have to grow accustomed to the sight of blood. Tell Matthew what I said."

"Yes, Papa," the boy said, running off down the hall as if chased by a wild bull.

Sam shook his head. The boy would never be strong enough to be a true Delamer. Not like Charlie would have been. Before he could think about the small blond-haired child killed by the Comanches, the pounding of heavy boots on the floorboards drew his attention.

Sam's brother Willie stood in the doorway. Bright red blood still flowed from a wound on the man's arm, dripping on the floor from time to time. Sweat had drawn long lines across Willie's dust-coated chest and forehead. His hair was matted and oily.

"Glad to see me?" Willie asked, glaring at his older brother.

"More than you might have cause to think," Sam said, waving his brother into the room. "We got problems that merit the attention of all the Delamers."

"Before you say anything else, you'd best know something. I mean to run this ranch," Willie said.

"If we don't do some fast thinking, there won't be a ranch to run," Sam said, handing the letters over to Willie.

Sam watched the expression change on his brother's face. At first there'd been the unmistakable livid pink of anger. The pink faded, leaving a deathly white. Willie's hands quivered, and Sam suspected his brother might faint. But the younger man's limbs grew firm, and his face regained its color.

"A dollar a head?" Willie asked. "Can we pay it?"

"Not a chance on this earth, Willie," Sam said. "The judge knows that."

"Then it's a move to take over the ranch?"

"Appears to be. Together with the canceling of the beef contract, I'd say it is for sure."

"Tell me, Sam, do you think it's because I shot that Yank major?" Willie asked, the earlier hostility fading away.

Sam smiled. If Willie thought it was his fault, he'd do whatever was necessary. But something warned him against pressing the advantage just then.

"No, I imagine the judge had been planning this for some time," Sam finally said.

"There's still the matter of the Cobbs," Willie said, handing the letters back to Sam. "Travis and his brother saved us from the Comanches yesterday, you know."

"Yes," Sam said. "I suppose it's best if we leave the market road open for their use."

"And no more dams on the creeks," Willie said. "I'd like that put in writing."

"You're learning," Sam said, smiling in a kind of begrudging admiration.

"And we'll be needing another agreement," Willie said. "One regarding the management of the ranch."

"Oh?" Sam asked, nervously shuffling his feet.

"Things've changed, Sam. You don't control this ranch anymore."

"Don't I?" Sam asked, raising his voice.

"No," Willie said. "I did as you said. I earned my keep.

99

I worked my tail off. More than that, I proved myself to the other men. They'll follow me. Can you say the same?"

"I pay their wages," Sam said, bitterly staring at the smile on Willie's face.

"And did you share their danger? Did you keep them from getting shot full of arrows and bullets?"

"Did you? Twelve of my men didn't ride back."

"We weren't fighting women and children," Willie said, glaring. "I heard all about your raid from Red Wolf. Shooting down babies doesn't require much courage. Just a very strong stomach."

It was Sam who shook now. He'd hoped to keep that episode from his brother's ears.

"That's past," Sam said. "What's more, most of the people around here are glad there isn't another generation of Indians camping on the Brazos."

"Most of the people around here have little gratitude for Sam Delamer," Willie said. "There are places you can't ride in safety. Papa never had that problem."

"Papa would have given away his own shirt," Sam said, smiling as he watched Willie's eyes fall self-consciously on his own bare chest. "But that doesn't help us out of our present difficulty. The ranch is mine, by deed and fact. But Franklin's dead. I need a foreman. The job's yours if you want it."

Willie didn't answer for a time. The anger wasn't completely gone. But a trace of a smile had surfaced.

"Look, Willie," Sam said, laughing inside as he realized he'd said the right thing. "We need you. You're the horseman in the family. Together we could make a fine team."

"I wish you'd said that when I first returned," Willie said. "I don't know if I can trust you now."

"If you can't trust your own brother, who can you trust?" Sam asked.

Willie didn't answer. The question was too painful, Sam thought. And there was a moment when he thought Willie might refuse the offer. But finally Sam extended his hand, and the younger Delamer clasped it firmly.

"Now, if you don't mind, write up the agreement for the Cobbs," Willie said.

Sam took out paper and wrote as Willie dictated. The agreement was witnessed by Willie and two of the hands. With the paper securely in his hand, Willie left the room. Sam gave the others a hard look, and they followed.

"Means nothing," Sam said as he closed the door of the room. "There was no money to buy them out anyway."

Sam then walked to the great map on the wall and looked over the lands stamped with the trident brand. The wonder of his dream crept back to him.

There was a danger, though, he reminded himself. The judge was a greedy man. An even greater threat rested in his younger brothers. James had a secretive look to his eyes, and Willie was downright dangerous. Riled, he was death on two legs.

James would soon leave for Houston to read for the law. And Willie? Sam bent over and scooped up the crumped telegram in his fingers. Well, there was always Johnson.

CHAPTER 14

Ψ

Willie walked up the stairs to James's room. He spoke to his brother about the fight with Red Wolf's Comanches, about his plans to run the ranch. Matthew brought in hot water, and Willie washed the dust and grime from his weary body.

"I'll bring some bandages for your arm," James said.

"Put them under a flame first," Willie told his brother. "And bring some whiskey."

"I didn't know you were a drinking man now," James said.

"It's for the wound," Willie said. "But it wouldn't hurt to warm my insides a little."

The two young men exchanged smiles. Then James disappeared.

As Willie cleaned the gash in his arm, it brought back other times to him again. Shiloh, The Wilderness, the dead and the dying.

"Are you all right?" James asked, walking through the door.

"Sure," Willie said, shaking away the memories.

Willie managed to get himself dressed and the wound bound. Then he took a horse from the stable and rode out to the Cobb farm. It was half a day's ride, but the eagerness in Willie's heart made the time pass quickly.

When Willie finally rode through the gate, he was greeted by a frowning Lester Cobb. The youth raised a shotgun and rubbed a bandaged hand as if to remind Willie of their earlier encounter. Willie ignored the young man and led Thunder on toward the house.

After tying his horse to the hitching post, Willie turned to find himself facing a second shotgun, this one held lightly by Art Cobb.

"Told you no Delamer's welcome on my land, boy," the man said.

"I remember," Willie said. "But I figured maybe that was changed. I thought I saw Trav yesterday out by our western boundary."

"I wouldn't even leave a snake to get itself scalped by Comanches," Mr. Cobb said. "Changes nothing."

"It changes everything," Willie said.

"Like fences?"

"More than fences," Willie said, handing the man the agreement he'd brought from the ranch. "No more dams or barricades in the road. Maybe now we can be neighbors."

The old man spread out the paper and read it carefully. A smile came to his face slowly. Then he set the gun aside and shook Willie's hand.

"Your pa'd be proud of you this day, Willie Delamer," Art Cobb said at last. "And I'd be pleased to have you stay to supper."

"I'd like that, sir," Willie said.

Willie and Ellen walked to a small hill that afternoon and watched the sunlight dance on the clear water of Bluff Creek. He felt warm with Ellen's soft head on his shoulder. Emotions awakened inside Willie which had been dead not long before.

"What will you do now, Willie?" Ellen asked as the sun slipped behind a large cloud.

"I'm not sure," he said. "I guess for now I'm the ranch foreman. That'll do. But we've lost the cattle contract for Fort Belknap, and Judge Fulton just set up a cattle tax. A dollar a head."

"Just for you or on everybody?" she asked, slipping away from his arms and looking deep into his eyes.

"I don't know," Willie said. "I suppose for everybody."

"We've got cattle on our place, Willie," she said. "So do most of the people along the river. Nobody has money to pay more taxes. We'll lose our land, our stock, everything."

Willie frowned as he realized it was true. There probably wasn't a hundred dollars spending money among all the little farms and ranches of the seven counties put together.

"We'll think of something," he said, cradling her head in his lap. "Now let me feel your hair against my cheek."

He leaned over and kissed her. It was a small enough thing, but it brought a ripple through his insides. He did it again. As he started to repeat the movement once more, though, Ellen stopped him.

"I'm sorry," Willie said, pulling back. "I didn't mean to take advantage."

"Willie, I've loved you since we were ten years old," she said. "But we both know better than to start something that will only have to end."

"I don't want it to end," Willie said. "I'll figure out something. I want you for my wife, Ellen Cobb. I won't ever feel for anybody what I feel for you."

"How do you know?" she asked, laughing. "I'm the only girl who's looked twice at you. You've been living with Indians and soldiers all your life. What do you know of women?"

"Do you want to hear of my exploits, Miss Cobb?" Willie asked. "Would you care to hear all about the fine young ladies in Richmond, the girl who nursed me to health in

Corinth? Or perhaps your taste leans more toward the loose morals of Memphis harlots and Red River temptresses."

"Stop it," she said, laughing. "I've heard it all from Travis. He's your friend, and a good one, but he's afraid of you, I think. He'd have me marry some careful little shopkeeper in Jacksboro."

"There's a lot to be said for that," Willie told her. "Ranchers have it hard."

"I'm no soft Shreveport dainty who's got to be combed and powdered and tended by five dozen maids," Ellen said. "I can outshoot half the men in Palo Pinto County. And I can outride my own brothers.

"You know me, Willie. I'm not suited to a life of ease. You build me a cabin along the river and find land to work and range for our cattle. That's enough for me."

"And me," he said, embracing her.

"But first there's the matter of the cattle tax," Ellen said.

"Well," Willie said, growing serious, "the answer's simple. You can't tax what's not there. We just have to get the cattle to market. There's a strong demand for beef in the North, but no railheads for shipping."

"The new railroad's most the way through Kansas," Ellen said. "I heard that in Jacksboro."

"But there's no getting cattle across the Indian territories between here and Kansas," Willie said. "There's Comanches and Kiowas in the western country, the civilized tribes to the east. I can't see the Kiowas giving us right of passage."

"Or the Comanches," she said, smiling.

"At least I can talk to them," Willie said.

They spoke no more about it for a time. The sun and the wildflowers were enjoyed, and a gentle breeze seemed to bring them closer together than he would have imagined that morning.

Mrs. Cobb had prepared a fine supper, and Willie found himself seated between Travis and Les. Ellen had been moved to the safety of her father's side. It didn't keep the two young people from exchanging smiles, though.

"That carpetbagger of a judge has set down a cattle tax," Ellen said as her mother sliced a beautiful apple pie.

"Cattle tax?" her father asked. "How much?"

"A dollar a head," Willie said. "We got a letter this morning all about it."

"Does Sam have the money?" Travis asked.

"Nobody has money like that," Willie said. "We must have five thousand head all rounded up and branded. And there's more on the range. There isn't five thousand dollars cash money in the whole of Texas."

"You plan to do anything?" Travis asked.

"Well," Willie said, smiling, "you can't tax what you can't see. We can either move the cattle to the far ranges or drive them to market."

"There are no markets around here," Art Cobb said. "And there's the cavalry to consider."

"I've fought Yank cavalry before," Willie said.

"Young'uns, you'd best take your leave," Mr. Cobb said, pointing to the three small boys and Ellen's sister Edna.

The children scattered. Then Mr. Cobb smiled.

"How's it best done, son?" the man asked Willie.

"You know we're talking about rebellion, don't you?" Willie asked.

"Didn't get enough of it in the Virginia hills, eh?" Mr. Cobb asked.

"Some'd say not," Travis said, laughing.

"It can't be open war, sir," Willie said. "They'd hang the lot of us. And it'd give 'em an excuse to take away anyone they took a dislike to. No, it'd have to be little things, and no killing."

"There's a better way," Les said, standing up. "I'm not saying this for you, Willie Delamer. I wouldn't lift a finger to save you or your brother. I say it because Ellen's got her heart set on marrying you, and because we got cattle ourselves.

"Pa, you know that old Cherokee we hired to tend horses?" Les asked, turning to his father. "Well, he was telling me about a trail north through the Nations. Called it Black

Beaver's trail, after some Indian chief. He said you could take it all the way to the Platte River if you had a mind to."

"And the Comanches and Kiowas?" Willie asked. "What do you do about them?"

"Son, you go fetch this injun," Mr. Cobb said to Les. "Let's hear it all."

They sat in silence as Les ran across the clearing to the barn. Shortly thereafter he returned with a weathered old man with leathery red skin.

"Tell them about Black Beaver's trail," Les said, pushing the Indian toward the table.

"What tribe are you?" Willie asked. "Cherokee?"

"Cherokee," the man said, nodding.

"And is there a trail north through the Nations?" Willie asked. "One passable for five or six thousand cattle?"

"If a man knows the way," the Indian said.

"And do you?" Art Cobb asked.

"As I know my nose," the Cherokee said, touching it with his finger.

"What are you called?" Willie asked.

"Two Bows," the man answered. "You will take the trail of Black Beaver?"

"Can you lead us?" Willie asked. "And will the Kiowas and Comanches allow us to pass?"

"They take to the buffalo valleys in summer," the Indian said. "Those who stay will steal cows. But you will pass."

"There's a cattle market in Kansas City," Willie said. "I hear they buy from farmers in Kansas. You know we can get five, six dollars a head up there. Maybe more."

"I read Chicago meat dealers were offering twenty to some breeders in Arkansas," Mr. Cobb said.

"You couldn't get that on a big herd," Willie said. "But it'd save us the tax and pay off our debts. We could raise enough men if we drove all the cattle from the valley up there in one herd. Would you go, Trav? And you, Les? We could even round up some of the boys from the regiment."

"Beats watching the grasses grow yellow," Travis said. "Les?"

"Somebody'll have to watch old Two Bows," the young man said.

Willie rode back to the ranch by the light of a quarter moon. It would have been a difficult thing for some, but Willie knew that land like an old friend. The horse stepped lively, too, and it wasn't yet midnight when Willie rode into the courtyard in front of the big house.

Willie had to wake Sam from his bed. He called James in as well and explained about Two Bows's trail.

"Do you trust this Indian?" Sam asked.

"More than some white men I've met," Willie said, a chill in his eyes.

"How long would it take to gather the men?" Sam asked.

"We'll have all we need inside a week," Willie said. "I already sent Trav out after some of the boys from the regiment. We'll drive the whole valley's cattle together. That way we'll pick up a lot of men who'd stay home otherwise."

"But if we just drove our own cattle . . ." Sam said.

"You could buy the other farms," Willie said, stamping his foot on the ground. "I won't go myself if you mean it to be like that. As for Two Bows, I think he'd be unlikely to go. You won't have enough men to drive the stock, either."

"Then that's how it will be," Sam said. "Can you organize the men, outfit them? Get the stock together?"

"With ease," Willie said.

"Then I'll wire the brokers in Chicago," Sam said. "They can get their agents to Kansas City. The judge can eat his taxes."

Sam was smiling in a cruel sort of way, and it brought a shudder down Willie's spine.

"I'll go," James said as they walked upstairs. "I can ride, and I've known cows all my life."

"And Houston?" Willie asked.

"It can wait," James said.

"No, James, you go to Houston," Willie said. "We'll need a lawyer more than a ranch hand to fight Fulton and his taxes. You leave the cattle to me. It's what I'm suited to."

"I know," James said. "But, Willie, watch out for yourself. I'll need your help to put things in order."

Willie paused and touched his brother's shoulder. It was the first time in the two weeks he'd been back that James leaned against him as he'd done as a boy. Willie brushed a strand of hair from the boy's eyes and smiled.

"Study hard, Jamie," Willie said. "I figure you'll have to be one heck of a lawyer to outfox that old carpetbagger and his cavalry."

"Watch out for Sam," James whispered as they reached the room.

"He's come around some," Willie said.

"You don't know him," James said. "He's trickier than a rattler."

"I've shot snakes in my time," Willie said.

They shared a brief laugh, then walked inside the bedroom.

In the days that followed, Willie worked like a madman. He was everywhere, organizing, getting men together, gathering stores and jerking beef. Travis Cobb returned with ten veterans of the war, and Sam contacted the Chicago beef buyers.

James left on a stage to Houston, laden down with copies of Judge Fulton's decrees and taxes in the hope of finding some fault in them as he studied.

So it was that the Delamers, each in his own way, sought to save their troubled ranch. And only the dark eyes of Sam Delamer and a telegram from Kansas City hinted of sinister motives.

CHAPTER 15

Ψ

Most every able-bodied man with a horse in the whole county assembled in the far western range of the Trident Ranch. There were grizzled veterans in butternut jackets and boys hiding slender shoulders in buckskins once worn by brothers or fathers. They carried revolvers designed by Colonel Colt or ancient muskets that might have seen action at San Jacinto.

There were a few new Sharps and Spencer's repeating rifles, and some of the men had adopted the fashion of wearing the broad-brimmed hats more common in the Rio Grande Valley. Mostly, though, the assemblage of men wore makeshift clothes of poplin and homespun cotton and wool, and carried firearms brought back from battle or taken down from over fireplaces.

Oddest of all was Sam Delamer. Sam was dressed in a deep blue waistcoat with shiny silver buttons. A broad white hat covered his head, casting dark shadows over his ruddy face. He carried at his side a fashionable black cane with a silver lion's head molded on the top.

Some of the veterans laughed at the sight. Between slugs of chewing tobacco Ted Slocum dubbed Sam the general.

"Reminds me of that Georgia general at Fredericksburg," Slocum said to the others. "You remember, Bates, the one with the big turkey feather in his hat."

Tom Bates, the crusty old vet who'd been hired to cook for the drive, nodded his head.

"Generals don't have much to do with what happens to a man, Slocum," Bates told his friend. "Remember, the major's with us."

Willie tried to ignore Sam. He knew the carriage and gaudy clothes irritated the men. Willie himself wore a simple cotton shirt and blue trousers. The old gray cavalry hat shaded his forehead, and a long-barreled army Colt rested in a holster on his hip.

That morning Willie stood beside his horse Thunder. To the other side stood Ellen Cobb. They watched Ellen's little brothers and sister playing in the back of her father's wagon. Travis and Les stood talking to their father about the journey. At their side was Two Bows, the Cherokee who would guide them up the trail.

Willie said little that morning. His thoughts were far away, somewhere past the Red River in the territories ceded to the Indian Nations. But Ellen was far from silent.

"Don't you think you could stay around for a month or two after being gone five years?" she asked.

"You know why I'm going," Willie said. "I could hardly stay with boys no older than fourteen riding along. Your own brother has a broken hand but he's on his horse. You wouldn't want a man who'd stay."

Her silence told him she knew he was right, but the look of longing in her eyes told him another story. There would be the emptiness, the long hours of missing and wanting and remembering.

There were no long good-byes for Willie. James had left, and he wasn't close to the other members of his family. He clutched Ellen's soft hands a moment and touched her hair. Then he turned to go.

111

The trail north of Palo Pinto County crossed vast stretches of buffalo grass and sagebrush. It was close to thirty miles to Jacksboro and close to another ten to the Trinity's western fork. The distance might be traveled by a lone rider in a single day, but a herd of five thousand cattle moved slowly. There was no point to running all the fat off a steer by pushing it up the trail.

There were clusters of farms along the Trinity, but much of the acreage between the Trinity and the Brazos was still inhabited by rattlesnakes and buzzards. A few ranches had run cattle there before the war, but Comanches and taxes had taken their toll.

Sam Delamer had bought up a few thousand acres in the southern part of Jack County, and the men bedded down the stock there that first night near three small springs. Water casks were filled, then dumped out in pools for the stock.

Watering the animals in such a manner was back-breaking work, and it was with no small relief that the Trinity was reached. A good crossing was found, and the herd was brought across bit by bit. There was time for a visit to Jacksboro by a few of the men. Then it was on to the Red River.

A Texas longhorn steer is one of nature's more pitiful creatures. Mostly horn and bone, its meat is tough and stringy, closer to buffalo than to the Jersey cattle a man could find on an Iowa farm. But no Jersey cow ever lived and died off buffalo grass and cactus. And no Jersey cow could have made the long trek from the Brazos to the Missouri at Kansas City or Sedalia.

The longhorn was a creature bred by the laws of survival, used to drought and heat and hardship. It was an ideal animal for driving across the barren wastes of the Indian Nations.

The long trail to Red River Crossing was little better. Great clouds of dust rose to choke a man, coating his skin like paint. That dust would clot the nostrils so that breathing was difficult. It would scratch at a man's eyes, blinding him and his horse so that he might ride into the wicked thorns of a black locust tree.

112

If the dust wasn't enough to kill a man, then heat was there to do it. The early summer days would swelter under the unrelenting sun. Temperatures of a hundred and ten degrees were common. When the winds blew, they brought little relief. Mostly they were dry, arid, blowing the choking dust against a man and howling like some ghostly spirit brought to life.

There were the cows, too. Willie'd never cared much for cattle, deeming them slightly smarter than chickens. They were contrary and nervous creatures who might scatter at the sound of a bell or the sight of a flash of lightning. The stupid beasts would walk right over a cliff or drown themselves in a creek three feet deep.

Dealing with a longhorn was no easy thing for a man on horseback. The beast didn't come by its name accidentally. Often the horns would stretch to as much as two and a half feet on each side of the head. A man had to keep himself and his horse safely clear of those horns while staying close enough to control the herd's movements.

Willie had started the drive off at a rather relaxed pace. As the days went on, the cattle were moved more and more of the daylight hours. Fatigue set in, and tempers grew short. By the time they approached the Red River, the band of cattlemen reminded Willie of the long marches before the hard fights at Chancellorsville and Spotsylvania.

But there were differences. There was no enemy riding around in a blue shirt, waving a saber or pointing a rifle. The enemy was the sun and the land and the cattle. And dying wasn't swift like in a battle. It was a lingering, blinding choking death that sapped a man's strength and robbed his spirit.

It wasn't all work and suffering, though. In the quiet of the evening as they sat around a campfire eating the last of Bates's stew and sipping a cup of muddy coffee made from boiled chicory, someone would laugh and start a story.

Sometimes there would be singing and even a little dancing. It would bring back a smile to Willie's tired face and life back to his weary bones. Most often he would sit away

113

from the fire with Travis and talk of Ellen. When not on night watch, young Brett Maxwell would join them. Sometimes Bates and Slocum would come over, and there would be a reunion of the old Comanche Raiders.

One night as Willie leaned against a gnarled old mulberry tree, Travis crept over beside him.

"What're you thinking on, Willie?" his old friend asked.

"The moon," Willie said, pointing to the big silver disk overhead.

"The moon?" Travis said. "Don't see it's any different than ever."

"That's what I was thinking," Willie said. "I must've looked at that moon a thousand times. I saw it the night I went up to the spirit cliffs with old Yellow Shirt and Red Wolf. I saw it every night when I was on the plains with the Comanches. I watched it rise out of the trees, shine right through the clouds that night before Shiloh."

"I don't remember any moon before Shiloh," Travis said. "Before Fredericksburg, maybe. We were awake on watch that whole night."

"Maybe it was," Willie said. "But I remember Shiloh better. I didn't sleep much that night. I'd been running dispatches, tired as I am right now. But I couldn't sleep. I kept thinking about how it could be my last night, and I didn't want to sleep it away.

"I saw the general that night, Trav, General Johnston himself. I got him a cup of chicory. We talked about Texas, about life out here. He told me about how he'd been a soldier most all his life. He'd been shot more than once. He fought in Mexico and Texas and was going to fight in Tennessee that next morning. But you know what he told me? He said it was a curse to be a soldier. He only had a handful of years that were peaceful. And all he ever wanted was that peace."

"What's that got to do with the moon?" Travis asked.

"Nothing really. It's just I started remembering it all. He died that next day. You remember. He was leading the charge in the Peach Orchard when they shot him. I keep looking

114

at that moon and thinking, Trav. I haven't known much peace in my life. None at all since I've been grown."

"There hasn't been much peace around here in quite a while," Travis said.

"Ellen said something to me about coming on this cattle drive. She asked me to stay a month or two. I've been gone so long, and we were just getting to know each other again."

"You know everything about her you need to know," Travis said. "And she knows all she wants to know about you."

Willie looked at the sourness that had come over the face of his friend.

"It won't always be like the last few years," Willie said. "I was sixteen before I ever shot at a man."

"You figure a thing like that changes, Willie? Your eyes don't show it. I saw how you looked when Sam sent you to work the horses. Willie Delamer, you're the best friend I ever had in this life. But I know you. You never in your life backed away from trouble, and that makes for a short life. Death follows you like fleas follow a dog."

"It's not how I want it," Willie said, spitting the juice from his tobacco at a sagebrush. "It's just how it is."

"And how it will be," Travis said, sighing. "Ellen doesn't see you that way much. She only remembers how you used to tell stories about buffalo and she-devils."

Willie laughed. It was what James had said.

"You figure you can make a life, the two of you?" Travis asked. "Grow corn in this hard country like Pa does?"

"And run cattle where corn won't grow," Willie said. "There are worse lives for a man."

"Can you put the wandering urge out of your mind?"

"I never had it there in the first place," Willie said. "I want more than anything to live along the river, make a place for myself and my sons to live. I want to tell them about their grandfather, about the ancient ones and old Yellow Shirt. Yes, about buffalo hunts and she-devils, too."

"And Sam?"

"I hope by the time this drive's through, he'll have a

different opinion of me. If I can put aside my saber, maybe Sam can put aside his."

"And if not?" Travis asked.

"Mary went to Colorado," Willie said, sighing.

"Can you?" his friend asked.

Willie stared at the moon above him. He remembered the question he'd put to the general. Why not stay in the beloved Texas hills if war was such a hated thing?

"No," Willie said. "I love the land enough to fight for it. And a man who won't fight for what's his doesn't deserve to call it his own."

"Then there'll be more fighting when we come back, Willie. And more dying. You'd make my sister a part of that?"

"I imagine I would," Willie said sadly. "But only if Sam forced it to be that way."

"Don't you see, Willie, it's never got to be that way."

"Doesn't it?" Willie asked.

The two friends stared at each other, a smile slowly coming to their faces.

"I suspect it does, knowing you like I do," Travis said. "And I wouldn't know you for a spineless sort of man. But you promised me about Ellen. You make your peace with Sam before you take her for your wife. I don't need a widow sister to look after all my days."

"I never thought a lot of getting myself shot, Trav, much less killed. What a hundred thousand Yanks couldn't do might be hard for Sam to get done."

The two old friends laughed after that, but it wasn't filled with joy. There was a tension to it. When Brett arrived with a guitar, Willie felt relived to be singing, even if it was camp songs from the war.

After they'd sung "Goober Peas," they joined in a rousing version of "The Yellow Rose of Texas" and "Dixie." A dozen other songs were thrown in for good measure. Then the wind picked up, and Willie motioned Brett to put aside the guitar.

"Morning comes early," Willie told them all. "And it won't wait on our singing."

CHAPTER 16

Ψ

Red River Crossing was reached the following afternoon. Long before the river was sighted, the cattle smelled the water. The animals moved forward at a faster pace, bawling and rumbling along so that the men became nervous.

Willie and most of the others had worked cattle before, though. The sight of a water frenzy was nothing new, and they simply moved the lead men to each side and left the lead steers to take the rest of the herd to the river.

The rest of the day was spent rounding up the cattle and confining them to a small area along the shore of the river. The dry spring weather had made the crossing easier, but the river bed was sandy, and spots of quicksand were marked so as to be avoided.

After struggling the better part of two days to get the cattle across the river, the men devoted a third day to swimming and enjoying the effects of some local Red River rum. It was little different from Art Cobb's corn liquor, but it brought a needed diversion for many of the men. Even Sam

Delamer left his isolated camp to the rear of the herd and joined in the merriment.

Willie himself sipped a cup or two of the brew, but he mainly sat back and laughed at the way the younger ones reacted to the liquor. There might have been those who would have denied the boys a turn at the jug, but Willie was not among them. If a boy was to take a man's load on his shoulders, then he was a man in all the ways that counted.

It had to be admitted that there was more than a little assistance needed to get some of the youngsters into their saddles, though. And Willie couldn't help smiling at their bloodshot eyes and wobbly legs. A Bible-toting fire and brimstone preacher couldn't have sworn as many men off liquor in a single night.

The country across the Red River was less hostile. There were low mountains on the horizon, and rivers cut the plain, providing stands of timber and plenty of water. Two Bows led the way, locating each day's camp beside a fresh mountain spring or freshwater creek.

Two Bows said the Nations had seen good rains that spring, for the creeks and rivers were full to their banks. It was a good sign, the Cherokee said. Good rains meant the buffalo hunting would also be good. That way the Comanches and Kiowas would keep to their hunting grounds farther west.

Not all the Indians were out chasing buffalo, though. Just past the Wichita Mountains Willie began noticing figures spying the herd. Guards were increased, and guns were cleaned and oiled.

Over a roaring campfire WIllie spoke to Two Bows of what he'd seen.

"I, too, have seen many shadows," the Indian said. "But there is little to fear. Since we crossed the Red River, we have been followed by many eyes."

"If we've been watched all that time, why didn't you say something?" Willie asked. "We should have kept a stronger guard."

"I will take you to Kansas," Two Bows said. "I would

119

not have you shoot children of the Wichita tribe who come to look at your fires. These who come now are Creek and Seminole. Soon we meet the Cherokee past the mountain. There we will treat."

"And these others?" Willie asked.

"There is no treating with such men," Two Bows said. "If a man rides to you and says that you ride upon his lands, then you treat with him. A man who hides his face behind trees is not a man to smoke with."

Willie smiled. In the words of the old Indian Willie found both truth and logic. It reminded him of his days in the camps of Yellow Shirt.

After crossing a river Two Bows identified as the Buffalo, a party of stone-faced men wearing bandanas on their foreheads and dressed in deerskin trousers and cloth shirts made their way through the broken ground to the camp of the cattlemen.

Two Bows smiled as the men approached.

"Cherokees," the Indian said proudly.

It didn't matter that the Indians who approached were calm and spoke in a civilized manner, though. The cattlemen were restless, and the sun glinted off more than one rifle.

The Cherokees themselves were hardly unarmed. They cradled rifles in their arms, and the tall man who appeared to be their leader shouted and gestured angrily.

"You come, Major," Two Bows said, waving Willie forward.

Sam reached the Indian ahead of him, though. Willie's brother shouted back at the Indians and flashed paper money in his hands. The Cherokees kept waving at the herd, but Sam just shook his head.

Two Bows walked between Sam and the other Indians. The scout spoke to the others calmly and with confidence. There was no excitement in his voice, and the situation quieted. No agreement seemed to be reached, though, and Sam was growing impatient.

Willie understood some of the words being spoken. There were similarities between Indian languages, and he spoke

120

a good deal of Comanche and Caddo. The Cherokees had their origins far to the east, though, and the languages were too different for Willie to follow the conversation.

"Tell them we mean to move northward," Sam shouted. "Tell them we'll pay to do so."

Two Bows stared at the paper money in Sam's hand. The chief of the Cherokees laughed at the bills. The Indians were growing agitated. The chief waved his rifle in the air, and the hillsides around them suddenly came alive. A hundred Indians surrounded the camp.

A hush filled the air. Even Sam Delamer grew silent. Among the assembled Indians were members of the Creek and Chickasaw tribes, together with the Cherokees.

"The chief wishes for payment," Two Bows whispered to Willie. "Many Texans cross the trail to Missouri across the Nations. Mostly they come east of this place. Chiefs don't trust paper money. They hold too much of the Confederate dollars. It is no good."

Willie smiled and nodded to the chief of the Cherokees. He could understand the lack of trust in Confederate bills.

"Tell him I would treat with him," Willie said. "Tell him we would smoke the pipe and shake hands."

The chief looked at Willie. In a movement of contempt the man shifted his eyes from Sam to the younger Delamer, staring at the gray cavalry hat on Willie's head.

"You served in the war against the federal government," the chief said, startling them all with his command of the English language. "I, too, fought this war. I rode with Stand Watie."

"I fought in Tennessee and Virginia," Willie said, clasping the Indian's hand. "I know you have no trust of paper, but we carry no gold. Is there something else you would take as payment? We don't wish to trespass on your lands. We would pay for right of passage."

"You have many cattle," the chief said. "They will eat much grass. You will leave fifty head for my people."

"Fifty head!" Sam shouted, pushing Willie aside.

"Leave this to me," Willie said, pulling his brother out

of the way. "He's a man of honor, and he'll be treated as such. If you'd dealt with Red Wolf in such a manner, a lot of bloodshed could have been prevented."

"Go back to your cows, little brother," Sam said.

Willie didn't bother to answer. He motioned to Bates and Travis, and the two men removed Sam from the scene.

"Fifty is too many," Willie said. "We must take these cows over hundreds of miles, and some will die. Many are needed so that we can pay the agents of the federal government. They place a heavy tax on our lands."

"You have much cattle," the chief said. "How can fifty be too many?"

"I wouldn't lie to you," Willie said. "We can pay no more than twenty-five steers. That will feed many people."

The chief stared long and hard at Willie. Then a smile came to his face.

"It will be as you say, Major," the chief finally said. "And you will keep your cows to the trail of Black Beaver."

"That will be done," Willie said.

The men sat down then and smoked tobacco. Willie gave a small canister of the stuff to the chief as a present, and Travis cut out twenty-five steers from the herd, following Willie's instructions that they should bear the trident brand in spite of Sam's objections.

After the Indians left, Sam confronted his brother over the agreement.

"You had no right to give away steers from my herd," Sam said angrily. "It was my place to deal with the Indians."

"You were doing such a fine job of it that we'd likely all end up dead," Willie said. "First of all, it's not your herd. Secondly it is my job to run this whole drive. That was settled before most of these men signed on. To tell you the truth, Sam, we only brought you along for the ride. You surely haven't shared the trail dust or the work."

Sam backed away from his brother a moment. Looking around at the faces of the men, it was clear Willie enjoyed their support and loyalty. Challenging him would be like taking on a cougar with a stick.

After dealing with the civilized tribes of the Nations, Willie found fewer eyes on the camps. Sometimes boys riding bareback on mustang ponies would run through the herd, shouting and laughing, but no harm was ever done.

Two broad rivers were crossed in the week that followed, the north and south forks of the Canadian. As the herd camped beside the south fork of the Cimarron River, though, a second body of Indians appeared.

It was clear even to the less experienced eyes among the trail hands that these weren't Cherokees or Creeks. The Indians were nearly naked, wearing only breechclouts and leggings. Their hair was short, sometimes braided, and they wore narrow spines of feathers across their heads.

"Kiowa," Willie whispered to Travis. "Supposed to be hunting buffalo."

The band of Indians, twenty or so in all, approached the herd cautiously. Willie motioned for Two Bows to follow, then spurred Thunder toward the intruders. Travis moved back, and Willie caught a glimpse in the corner of his eye of Bates and Slocum gathering the men in a defensive position between the Kiowas and the herd.

When Willie came close to the Indians, the leader of the Kiowas raised his hand in a sign of peace. Willie matched the movement. Two Bows tried out some Cherokee words on the man, but they had no effect. Then Willie spoke, saying words he'd learned in the Comanche camps many summers before.

Willie spoke to the Kiowa for several minutes. Then Willie looked at the faces of the younger members of the Kiowa band. Some were barely twelve, yet signs of hunger and desperation were in their eyes. Willie looked at the yellowing teeth, at skin stretched tight over ribs, eyes set deep in their sockets. He couldn't help but sigh.

Bad times had come to the Kiowas of late. Cheyennes had been pushed southeast by settlers and were roaming the valleys of the Cimarron and Republican rivers. The Comanches and Kiowas were caught between the Texans to the south and their fellow Indians on the east, north and west. There wasn't enough food for all.

Willie shouted for another twenty head to be cut from the herd.

"These will keep your bellies full through the snows," Willie told the Indians.

"You have many more cows," the Kiowa chief said. "You can give us many more."

"These are not your lands," Willie said, frowning at the man. "They belong to others who have been paid for right of passage. You are hungry, so I give you beef. We don't fear you, and we'll give you battle if you like."

Willie paused to open his shirt and reveal the jagged lance scar on his upper arm and the smaller knife wound received in combat with the Comanches that very year.

"I have fought the Comanches," Willie told the man, pointing to the scars. "I have fought the blue coats, too. I don't fear the Kiowa. I give you cows so that your little ones might not know the pain of hunger in their bellies as I have. But if you mean to have war, then I will give it to you."

Willie backed away, but the Kiowa chief motioned for him to stay.

"Then we will smoke on this," Willie said, taking the pipe from Two Bows. "And there will be peace between us."

The Kiowa chief nodded, and shouts filled the air.

That should have been the end to the clashes between red men and white men on the drive, but such was not the case. Amid the deepest black of night the stillness was broken by the firing of a rifle.

It was the signal of the night watch, and Willie drew out his Spencer's rifle and raced to the horses. Brett Maxwell was at his side, and the two were jointed by Bates and the Cobb brothers seconds later.

"Bates, get the camp secured," Willie said to the crusty old veteran. "Les, stay with him. You two follow me," he said then, pointing to Travis and Brett.

The ride to the outer fringe of the herd took only a few minutes. Young Lige Hannah had been on guard duty, and the boy now lay on the ground, a great bloody gash in his fourteen-year old skull. Willie waved for two others to join their group, then started down a small slope toward the sound of cattle being driven away from the main herd.

"Never figured raiders in this country," Travis whispered as they rode.

"Got to be Indians," Willie said. "Likely our friends the Kiowa. That chief had a well fed look to his face. A man that would let children starve would hardly keep his word to a white man."

It wasn't long before Willie got his proof. In the moonlight before him seven Indians were moving thirty cattle toward the west. Waving two others to each side, Willie took out his rifle and drew a bead on the nearest Indian.

The others stared in surprise as Willie fired twice rapidly, striking in turn the nearest Indians. Both clutched their chests and fell lifeless to the ground. The other men abandoned the cattle and tried to escape. Travis got one with his pistol, and two others were cut down from the other side in a gully. The chief turned and stared as Willie held him in his sights. Then the trigger was squeezed, and the fat man rolled off his horse and was trampled by the excited cattle.

The remaining Indian, a young man of fifteen or so, was dragged to Willie. With cold eyes feverish with anger, Willie spoke to the boy his Comanche words.

"I'll feed a man who's hungry, lift him up if he's fallen from his horse. But if he makes false talk with me," Willie said, "I'll ride three moons to see him dead."

Willie pointed his rifle at the young man and watched the Indian's eyes fill with fear. The rifle discharged, and the bullet hit the ground an inch from the boy's foot.

"Tell my words to your people," Willie said. "I won't ride down on your people in their sleep as you would do to me. I won't take your cows, for your little ones are hungry. But if you stalk my trail, if you harm my men, then I will bury all of you."

The Indian's eyes told WIllie that he understood. In a great haste the boy rode away, the dust from his trail clouding the air.

"Let's get back to camp," Willie said, spreading out the men in order to drive the stolen cattle back to the herd.

Willie found no sleep that night. He avoided Travis's eyes, remembering what his friend had said about death following Willie. But the thing that had been done was necessary. And it was what Bill Delamer would have done.

CHAPTER 17

Ψ

Following the night raid by the Kiowas, Sam retreated to his ledgers and the shade of the carriage. Willie began riding through the camps as he'd once rode through regiments and brigades in Virginia. The former major could be seen setting the night watches, rounding up strays, joining in the singing and wrestling that followed supper.

As the herd crossed the Kansas border, sadness struck. Young Lige Hannah, suffering from the effects of his head wound, became feverish and died. His brother Amos read the burying words over the grave, and wildflowers were set beside a wooden plank etched with the boy's name.

Hard men stood beside the grave, tears in the corners of their eyes. Death was never far from any of them, but fourteen was a tender age for life to end. It would have taken a heartless man to feel nothing.

No tears came from Willie. Crying was a thing put behind him long ago. The sadness was felt, though, and Willie changed the night watches so that the younger members of the company were matched with veterans.

Willie paired himself with Brett Maxwell. Brett had proven himself against the Comanches back at the Trident, and Willie felt at ease with the young man. It meant surrendering the pleasant evenings spent with Travis Cobb, but Willie knew Travis felt better looking out for his brother Les.

While the new arrangement drew some grumbling, most of the men felt better about things overall. As they camped along the banks of the Arkansas River, only a couple of hundred miles separated them from their destination at Kansas City. And thoughts of money and liquor, women and excitement lifted their spirits.

That night there was another feeling in the air, though. Thunder shuddered nervously, and Willie felt an uneasiness creeping up his spine. The wind picked up, and the cattle stirred.

"Something wrong?" Brett asked as Willie turned his horse's head and started toward a patch of woods in the distance.

"Pull out your rifle and keep your ears open," Willie said. "Could be someone's out here."

"Wolves?" young Maxwell asked, loading his rifle as he closed the distance between himself and Willie.

"Not enough noise for animals," Willie said. "But it could be a party of Indians come for a look."

Willie slowed to allow his young partner to join him. Then the two of them rode cautiously out toward the woods, searching all the while for some sign of an intruder.

It wasn't long in coming. Just ahead of them a tree shook. Willie leaned over his horse to present a smaller target as he moved forward to investigate. His ears picked up the heavy breathing of horses, and he motioned Brett to halt.

"Just ahead," Willie whispered. "If they start shooting, get to those rocks to the right and let your horse go."

"Shouldn't we fire a warning shot?" Brett asked. "Let the others know we're out here?"

"Not unless you're anxious to have a stampede," Willie said. "The cows've been skittish all night."

Two figures emerged from the darkness then, and Willie called to them.

"Hold there!" Willie called out. "Who are you?"

The answer was a rapid series of pistol shots which shattered the stillness of the night and excited the cattle. Willie and Brett rode like fury for the rocks as rifle bullets tore into the ground all around them. Loud shouts were heard from the woods, fragmented sentences that stunned Willie. These men spoke English. They were rustlers.

"Behind the rocks!" one of the thieves cried out.

Two more rifles barked, and bits of rock flew into the air. Willie waved his hat at Thunder, and the horses raced back toward the herd. The cattle themselves were moving into the river, bawling and stomping.

"How many you figure are out there?" Brett asked as another rifle shot flashed out into the night.

"Maybe a dozen," Willie said. "Keep your head down. Help will be coming."

But no one came for a long time. The shadows creeping out of the woods came closer, and Willie made sure his guns were fully loaded.

"Now listen to me, Brett Maxwell," Willie finally said. "It's too dark to see anything. The best chance you have to hit something is to fire at a man's gun flash. When you shoot your own gun, roll to one side. Don't get yourself caught flat-footed. It's as easy to get yourself killed by a man who doesn't see you as by one who does."

Brett nodded, then slipped along the side of the rocks opposite Willie. Willie himself followed two shadows less than a hundred yards away. When one of them fired, Willie opened up with his Spencer's, spraying the two men with four rapid shots.

Two cries followed, and no more firing came from that quarter. The moans of the two wounded men upset the others, too. The shooting became more sporadic. But Willie found no comfort in that. The herd was threatening to stampede, and the rest of the night watch would be busy with the stock.

"When will they come, Willie?" Bret asked, dodging two shots that kicked up spirals of dust behind them.

"They're behind us," Willie said, rolling over just as the rock in front of him exploded in a hailstorm of fire.

There wasn't time to think. Guns were going off seemingly everywhere, and the air was full of bullets. Willie fired his rifle, finding his target more than once. But there were more of the rustlers, and two bullets nicked Willie's left shoulder.

Willie rolled over against the rocks, dropping his rifle. Pain throbbed from the more serious of the wounds, a bullet lodged against his collarbone. His left arm was limp, but in his right he held a Colt revolver. The first man to approach him was blown to eternity, and two others beat a hasty retreat.

"Brett?" Willie called as his eyes grew cloudy.

The heavy breathing of the young man beside him was his only answer. But he could hear blood dripping on the ground.

"Come on!" Willie screamed, blinking to clear his eyes. "Finish it!"

The shadows came no closer, though. The sound of pounding hooves shook the ground, and the rustlers tried to scatter. There was no time, though. Bodies fell left and right, and others threw down their guns and begged for mercy.

Willie's eyes cleared. He stuck the pistol back in his holster and pulled Brett to his side. The young man's eyes were closed, and his breathing was shallow. Willie propped Brett's shoulders up and spoke softly.

"It's all right now," Willie said as he had many times before to other young men. "The fighting's over."

The young man's eyes cracked open, and a smile came to his lips.

"Where'd they hit you?" Willie asked.

"Here and there," Brett said, tearing open his shirt so that Willie could see the three holes in the pale flesh of the boy's chest. And yet the worst of the bleeding came from a big hole in the right leg of the young man.

While the horsemen rounded up their prisoners, Willie tore strips from his shirt and bound Brett's leg. The bleeding slowed, and the boy's eyes brightened. Then a shudder wound through Brett's shoulder, and Willie grew cold. The young man's eyes grew wide and white, and his breathing ceased.

"No!" Willie shouted, shaking the body of his young friend. "Not again!"

But Brett had already passed from the world of the living, and nothing could bring him back.

Travis knelt at Willie's side and began treating the two holes in Willie's shoulder. Even the pouring of alcohol into the open wounds failed to stir the ex-major's feelings.

"Willie, one of them bullets is still in there," Travis said.

"Get Bates to cut it out," Willie said. "He's got the best hands in the regiment."

"Regiment?" Travis asked. "Willie, you know where you are?"

"Where I am?" Willie asked, confused.

Between the pain from his shoulder and the blood all around him, it came back to him.

"Brett's dead," Willie said at last. "Just like all the others."

Travis helped Willie to his feet after binding the wounds. Willie stepped lightly, then froze. Looking down he found himself standing in a pool of blood. His stomach turned, and he grew faint.

"Willie?" Travis asked.

"I'm all right," Willie said, shaking the dizziness from his head. "You think you can get me on a horse?"

"Seems like I've done it before," Travis said, allowing Willie to lean against him.

The herd was held up two days at the Arkansas. Bates took the bullet from Willie's shoulder and dressed the two wounds. There were others among the company who'd caught bullets, and several of the rustlers, too.

When the outlaws were well enough to travel, Travis had

them put in the back of the supply wagon. A half-dozen men escorted them into Wichita and handed them over to a federal marshal.

Brett Maxwell was taken to Wichita, too. It was Sam's idea. It didn't seem fitting to bury him together with men who'd been shot robbing the herd, and Mrs. Maxwell would rest easier knowing her son was lying in a proper church-yard.

Willie found time to congratulate Bates on his doctoring. The scars would hardly show. At least they wouldn't be noticed by others with all the rest of the marks on his chest and shoulders.

Although his muscles were still stiff and sore, Willie could walk well enough to move around. He urged the herd into motion, and soon the cattle were once again winding their way up the trail to Kansas City.

CHAPTER 18

Willie didn't feel strong enough to spend the whole day in the saddle, so he rode briefly, then sat down next to Bates at the head of the cook's wagon. The herd was moved across the Arkansas, and for a time things settled down.

It didn't last, though. Before they'd gotten any great distance from the river, a small body of men appeared carrying shotguns. In their midst was a tall man wearing the badge of a law officer.

"Howdy there," the sheriff said, tipping his hat to them. "Might I ask where you be bound?"

"Driving beef to market," Willie said, stepping down from the wagon and walking slowly to where the men stood.

"Longhorns to Sedalia, eh?" one of the men said. "Just like we figured."

"Kansas City," Willie said.

"Makes no difference," the sheriff said. "Fraid you cain't move them cows through here. Best find another way."

Willie turned to Two Bows.

"Is there another way?" he asked the Indian.

"North to the Kansas River," Two Bows said. "East from there."

"That's a hundred miles out of the way," Willie said. "There's got to be some way to come through here. We'll pay for the right of way."

"Texas cows been coming through here for years," the sheriff said. "Every single time they pass, our stock dies off with the Texas fever."

"Our stock carries no fever," Willie said. "Judge for yourself. They're healthy as ever."

"Don't bother Texas beef," the sheriff explained. "Just kills all the others."

Willie started to argue, but two of the Brazos men stopped him.

"He's telling the truth, Major," a man named Small said. "I was through here a few years back. We near fought a war to get through."

"We ain't afraid of a little fighting, are we, Major?" someone else said. "'Specially of no bunch of Jayhawk farmers."

"Hold your horses," Willie said to the men. "We didn't come here to do any killing. There's been enough of that. Sheriff, we'll pay for any damage done."

"We heard that before," one of the farmers said. "You Texans don't pay for a man's stock all dying off. No, you keep your distance."

Willie frowned. Looking at the faces of the men in front of him, he saw they weren't violent men. They probably had families. But they were determined to protect their homes, and others likely waited to join them up the trail.

"We have to get these cattle to market," Willie said. "Without the money, we'll lose our homes. Everything we own is tied up in this herd. And there are boys who've died on this drive, one only fourteen."

"There'll be more if you try to come through," the sheriff said. "I care more about my own family, my friends. You can drive your cows back into the Nations and eat'em for all I care."

Willie turned and looked at the other cattlemen. It seemed as if all their plans had turned sour.

"We'll be watching you Texans," the sheriff said, motioning for the others in his party to withdraw. "Consider yourself warned. Any man or cow turns east from here is fair game."

Willie stared at the sheriff with bitterness. As the farmers turned away, he kicked the ground hard.

"Make camp here tonight," Willie said to the men. "we'll figure out something."

For the first time Willie read doubt in the faces of the other men. Worse, he felt it in his own heart. Willie knew nothing of the land in front of them except that to the east lay an angry mob of Kansas farmers prepared to blast them with shotguns. The Platte River was supposed to be somewhere north of them, and after that, the Missouri.

That night they sat beside their campfire and stared at the pinpricks of light that dotted the eastern horizon.

"They're just out there waiting," Willie said, "ready to blow us to pieces if we try to move. And there's not much chance of hiding five thousand cows."

"No, I expect not," Travis said.

As they looked at the cloudy sky overhead, the stillness was shattered by sounds of gunfire.

"They're back," Willie said, throwing a plate of beans in the fire. "Get your guns!"

It was no raid this time, though. Some of the more daring of the Kansas farmers had decided to settle the question once and for all. Seven riders had hit the eastern flank, and now the whole herd was racing back toward the Arkansas River in a furious stampede.

There was little time to react. Each man made a desperate grab for his horse and gun. In a moment they were mounted and riding. But turning five thousand crazed cattle was no simple task. And if the herd scattered, it would take all summer to get the cattle rounded up.

Willie got onto the back of old Thunder and rode out toward the herd. With Travis and Les Cobb behind him,

135

the three fired revolvers and strained to cut off the cattle. The objective was to turn the stampede into a big circle and bring the animals back to where they'd started.

With five thousand head and only a handful of experienced drovers, though, it soon became clear that wouldn't happen. Worse, the skies were now afire with lightning, and the cattle raced from the violent thunder that shook the ground.

Willie pulled up and watched the cattle run away from them.

"Get to the other side, Trav," Willie yelled to his friend. "Try to get the herd pinched in on the flanks. We'll run 'em back to the river."

Travis nodded, then spurred his horse off into the night. Soon the riders who'd been facing the cattle and trying to cut them off peeled off to the sides. The sole task ahead of them now was to control the herd, keep it together.

It was not an easy thing for all the men to get out of the way of the herd, though. Willie saw two riderless horses as he galloped along the left flank. Seconds later terrifying screams could be heard as men were trampled.

Then, as if by magic, a bolt of lightning did what the men had been unable to. An explosion of flame erupted on a hillside directly ahead of them, and the cattle shifted their run back toward the original camp.

"How far can they run before stopping?" Willie cried out.

But no answer came, and there was no time to wait for one. The six men around Willie spread out and began cutting the herd, slicing off bits of it to control. And fatigue had set in, too. The rear of the herd began slowing, and for the first time it looked like the drive might be saved.

Willie's shoulder ached and burned, but he wouldn't stop. Poor Thunder was in a heavy lather, near worn down by the hard riding up the trail and now by the stampede. But as Willie eased up on the reins and let his horse slow to a trot, he saw something which brought a shudder to his insides.

In the path of the cattle lay the camp. The tall cook's wagon was already rolling into motion. Bates had somehow managed to get the team hitched by himself and was even now driving the horses like fury.

The dark carriage of Sam Delamer remained idle, though. It would have been easier for Willie to assume Sam had climbed onto the wagon and was headed for safety. But he thought he spotted a shadow beside the carriage.

Willie spurred Thunder on, straining to beat the cattle to the carriage. His horse was spent, though. Sliding his rifle into a leather scabbard behind his saddle, Willie halted the horse, slid off the saddle and grabbed a nearby mount.

It had been years since Willie'd ridden a saddleless horse. There was panic in his movements, though, and he didn't think about it. The fresh horse ran with the wind, and Willie circled the herd, racing to beat the cattle to Sam's carriage.

As he urged the horse onward, it was all he could do to hold on. His left arm was near useless. His fingers were numb, and the shoulder throbbed with pain. But he kept the horse moving with his knees.

Willie reached the carriage about a hundred yards ahead of the cattle. He halted the horse by pressing his knees against the animal's ribs, then stretched out his right hand to Sam.

Willie's older brother stood beside the carriage holding two ledgers. He started to argue with Willie over something, but the earth shook with the oncoming fury of the stampede. Sam dropped one ledger, stuffed the other in his trousers and grabbed his brother's hand.

"Let's get out of here," Sam said as Willie pulled him up on the horse.

"Didn't have it in mind to wait around," Willie said, urging the horse into motion.

As they galloped away, Willie could hear the crash of the carriage. By the time they reached the safety of a small hill, nothing could be seen of the carriage amid the sea of crazed cattle.

"You all right?" Willie asked as they stared at the ravaged camp below them.

"Fine," Sam said.

"It's been a long time since we've been on a horse together," Willie said.

"Not since we were boys," Sam said.

"More than ten years," Willie said. "Twelve, I believe."

"Might be," Sam said, sliding off the rear of the horse.

"My eighth summer," Willie said. "You'd come back from that school for a time, all fancy in your New Orleans shoes. And me, I was barefoot and bareback, skinnier than a rail fence."

"Not much point remembering things like that," Sam said.

Willie frowned. Blood dripped through the bandages on his shoulder, and he grew light-headed. He swallowed, though, and said what came to his mind.

"What I was thinking about, Sam, was how we didn't used to be so far from each other," Willie said. "There was a time when I'd run all day just to see you."

"Things change," Sam said, laughing. "To tell the truth, I was surprised you rode down there to pull my fat out of the fire."

"Then I'm sorry," Willie said. "I'd have it known that my brothers can count on me when there's trouble."

"I guess they know that," Sam said. "You saved the herd for sure."

Willie looked down at the weary cattle below. It had started raining, and Willie shivered with cold.

"That doesn't matter just a whole lot, does it?" Willie asked his brother. "What with the market roads barred, I don't see we've got a lot of chance to sell the cattle."

"I didn't know you were handling the business end of things, too, Willie Delamer. I tell you what. You keep this herd in one piece long enough for me to ride to Wichita. You do that and keep the hands from shooting any Kansas farmers, and we'll bring that cattle market to us."

"Bring it to us?" Willie asked.

138

"Well, if we can't get through to Missouri, it's for sure nobody else will. And they're hungry for beef in Chicago. I imagine that cattle agent won't mind finding another railhead for us."

"You'll need a good horse to take you," Willie said. "Borrow Thunder. That horse could ride through a hailstorm."

"I'll take your word at that. And I'll borrow Two Bows to get me to Wichita. You tend the rest."

"I will," Willie said, smiling for the first time in days despite the pain in his shoulder.

As his brother walked away, Willie stumbled to the cook's wagon. Bates was playing a mouth organ and watching the rain spatter around his feet.

"Bates, you got a free hand?" Willie asked.

The cook smiled and turned toward Willie.

"Major?"

"I think maybe you'd best rebind that shoulder of mine," Willie said, opening his shirt so that Bates could see the red smear of blood covering the left side of his chest.

"Get in the back of the wagon, Major. By gum, you've opened the whole blessed thing up. A man who's seen bullet wounds ought to know better."

Willie climbed into the back of the wagon and collapsed. As Bates began cutting away the bandages and poking into the wound, the throbbing increased. Willie felt his eyes cloud, and a weariness dulled his senses.

"Wound's still clean, Major," Bates told him.

But Willie didn't hear the words. The fatigue had been too much for him.

"You rest easy, Major," Bates said. "Sleep's a tonic, too."

CHAPTER 19

It was three days before Sam returned from Wichita. A new black carriage had been purchased, along with a fresh suit of clothes. To be truthful, Sam returned to the herd more like some foreign monarch than the part owner of a stranded herd of Texas longhorns.

The three days had been used to good advantage. The herd had been put back together, minus a hundred or so strays that had wandered hopelessly far from camp. Scrapes and bruises were patched and bandaged. And two more graves had been dug.

Willie turned over the herd to Travis Cobb. The wound in his shoulder had brought a fever, and he couldn't safely sit a horse. Willie devoted his energies to trying to keep the men from riding out and lynching the farmers who'd started the stampede.

"Murder, pure and simple," Slocum had said. "We ought to empty a few Kansas saddles."

The men were mostly in agreement, but Willie hushed the talk of revenge.

"We've got enough trouble," he told the men. "But we double the night watches. If they mean to test us again, then it won't be our men that do the dying."

The chill that came to Willie's face silenced the argument. Some of them had seen that look before.

Sam's return left no time for further thoughts of revenge anyway. The man, wearing a fine new white hat and black coat, had a smile on his face ten feet wide.

"Willie, tomorrow we head the steers north," Sam said.

"Then you talked to the cattle agent?" Willie asked.

"Over the telegraph," Sam said. "The man plans to meet us in Abilene. That's fifty miles closer than overland to Kansas City. And he says he can handle the entire herd."

"Where's Abilene?" Willie asked. "Due north?"

"Some east," Two Bows told them. "Easy driving."

"Maybe a hundred miles in all," Sam told the men. "Ten days."

The men whooped and hollered. And although there was no such thing as easy driving when five thousand cattle were involved, the trail to Abilene was covered with a speed brought by the anticipation of a long journey's end.

Abilene itself wasn't much of a town. Built along the Kansas River west of Fort Riley, it had grown up as a market for farm goods and a supply depot for the railroad. Small shops and stores clustered in one part of town while a line of saloons and gambling houses left from the building of the railroad made up the remainder.

The cattle agent waited for them outside of town. Makeshift corrals had been put up, and boxcars waited on the nearby tracks. As fast as the steers and cows could be counted, they were run through the corral and loaded on the cars. By mid-afternoon the first trainload of cattle was rolling eastward to Kansas City.

In truth the only big problem in accounting for the cattle was keeping a clear tally of who the stock belonged to. Brands had to be checked and recorded, and it was no easy task. Some of the men on the drive had brought along handfuls of steers. Others, like the Cobbs and Harrells, had a hundred or so each. The rest bore the trident brand of the Delamer family.

It was bitterly disappointing to some of the men to discover that their dozen or so cattle hadn't survived the journey. Willie would have paid the small ranchers anyway, but Sam was handling the money.

"Everyone took the same risk," Sam said as he meted out the money.

For those like Travis Cobb, six dollars a head marked down ninety-two times spelled a small fortune. The Trident's share amounted to well over twenty-five thousand dollars.

"Enough to buy a dozen Yank judges," Sam said, smiling. "Even after paying off the men."

The hands had been promised fifty dollars for the drive, but a generous Sam Delamer paid seventy-five. After all, only fourteen of the original hands remained. Those with wives, like Bates and Slocum, started the long ride back to Texas that very night. Others stayed to celebrate. Seventy-five dollars bought a lot of women and whiskey in Abilene.

Sam and Willie took rooms in the Kansas Hotel, up on the second floor away from the noise of the street. Baths were enjoyed, and fried potatoes and an ocean of vegetables were eaten for dinner.

That night Willie took a crisp twenty from the ranch's profits and walked across the street to the Silver Dollar, a popular bar and gaming house where Travis was playing cards. A local construction boss for the railroad and two gentlemen from town joined them in a friendly game of low stakes poker.

A piano blared behind them. Smoke from cigars and handrolled cigarettes swirled around oil lamps hung from the ceiling. Women wearing high stockings and low-cut dresses draped their arms around men and laughed at their crude suggestions.

"There's talk of building a depot for cattle here in Abilene," one of the gentlemen said to Willie. "You think Texans would drive cattle up here instead of to Sedalia or Kansas City?"

"Don't see why not," Willie said. "The trail's narrow, and there's no problem with the farmers in the eastern part of the state."

"Still Indian trouble," the man said. "We find Kiowas and even Cheyennes in the southern part of the state, not to mention in the Nations."

"We had a little trouble ourselves," Travis said. "But we buy up a few of those repeating rifles, and the tribes'll keep their distance."

"Well, there's money to be made in beef cattle," the railroad man said, exposing a hand that held three kings. "People in the East are hungry for beef. A lot of people let their herds dwindle during the war. They're reluctant to slaughter cows for food."

"If there was a market in Abilene, I imagine you'd see a lot of Texas herds," Willie said. "There are thousands of longhorns scattered over open range from the Pecos to the Trinity. Men are out of work, what with no money to be found, and the promise of hard cash would bring'em running."

"That's excellent news, young man," the first gentleman said. "My name's Barton. I run the bank in town. This is my brother-in-law, Henry Lawton. He owns the emporium."

Willie extended his hand to each in turn.

"I'm Willie Delamer," he said.

"Not the one who owns the Trident Ranch?" the third man, the railroader asked.

"Part owner," Willie said. "I've got two brothers."

"You're the younger, I gather," the man said. "I spoke with your brother Sam about investing in railroads."

"I'm younger by several years, sir," Willie said. "But no less a Delamer."

Travis nodded his head, and a murmur of agreement sprang up from the cattlemen at the bar.

"Well, I expect we'll be talking more about railroads," the man said. "There are plans to extend the southern lines out of Marshall soon. Southern railroads are selling cheap right now. Panic selling. Your brother seems interested in a line running west along the Brazos."

"It'd be good for business," Willie said. "But I suspect it would take a lot of men to put a line through to Palo Pinto County. And I can't see the purpose of it. Nobody much lives out there to speak of."

"Now," the railroad man said. "There weren't many people along the Kansas until commerce began to flow. First the wagon trains. Now the railroad. Soon enough this country will be crisscrossed with track like it is with rivers. New highways for people and goods."

Willie frowned. He suspected it wouldn't be so long before towns and people covered even the old buffalo valleys of the Comanches.

"That doesn't seem to please you, young man," Barton observed. "You don't care for towns?"

"Never thought about it much," Willie said. "I grew up in hard country where a man mostly fought the land to survive. Then lately it seems like a man's got to fight other men just to be left alone."

"I noticed your hat," the railroader said. "You fought for the South, I gather."

"Yes, sir," Travis said, shuffling the cards. "Major of cavalry in General Hood's Brigade till the general went down to Tennessee. Fought in the Shenandoah, at Gettysburg, was with General Lee when the peace was signed at Appomattox."

"I fought in the war, too," the railroad man explained. "Colonel of Missouri volunteers. Amos Courtney. And any man who fought in Virginia ought to know the only way to keep it from happening all over again is to tie this country together tight. And that's best done by the railroads."

"Maybe," Willie said.

"Your brother thinks so," Colonel Courtney said. "He told me he planned to buy into our line ten thousand dollars worth."

Willie's eyebrows raised. Sam's third didn't come to that much.

"Surprise you, son?" the colonel asked. "I didn't get a hint from your brother that he had any partners in his business."

"He sometimes forgets," Willie said. "I have to remind him."

They played cards most of that evening. Willie smiled as he watched the way the colonel played cards. You could tell a lot about a man by the way he gambled. The colonel would wait for the right hand, then put everything behind it. The banker and his brother-in-law would try to stick to a sure thing. They would never call a hand backed by a big wager.

Travis played hunches. If he felt he would draw to a straight or a flush, he'd bet that way. Willie would only risk his profits, once they were made. And he was careful never to play out a hand that held no promise.

The following evening the five men sat down together again. Willie was surprised the banker had returned. Barton had lost two hundred dollars the night before, and such losses were out of character for a man of his profession. But it soon became clear that Barton was courting the colonel's interests. The brother-in-law was along for the ride.

The play that night was more heated. Willie had argued with Sam over the investments, angry that the family's money should be risked without consulting all concerned. Willie turned his anger on the colonel, forcing the man into pots where he didn't belong, calling bluffs and playing to advantage. By nine o'clock the railroader had lost two thousand dollars.

"You out for the man's blood, Willie?" Travis asked as they went to the bar for a new deck of cards. "You're bleeding the man."

"He's got more," Willie said. "I mean to show him who he'd be dealing with besides Sam."

But as they played on, Willie noticed a glimmer of pleasure brightening in the colonel's eye. Barton and Lawton had withdrawn, and Travis, reaching the break-even point, had cashed his chips as well.

145

"I do enjoy playing with you, Major," Courtney said. "You do everything like you play cards?"

"Some might say so," Willie said.

"Interesting style," the colonel said. "Attack right up front. But you never can tell when something's being held in reserve. Makes it a challenge to beat you."

"I haven't been beaten many times, Colonel," Willie said. "Delamers never were good losers. You might be able to kill a few of us, but you'd never get away with putting us under your thumb. It's downright dangerous."

"Tell me, does your brother play cards?"

"He'd rather read his ledgers," Willie said, laughing. "But he's a hard man in his way. I wouldn't plan on doing business with him to your advantage. He'll likely end up with your shirt."

"If I don't lose it to you first," the colonel said, smiling.

Willie finished that night's game another two thousand ahead. Colonel Courtney handed over a bank draft to cover his losings and promised another game the next day.

It was close to noon when Willie finally rolled out of bed the following morning. After depositing the draft in Barton's bank, he treated the men from the drive to dinner at the hotel and drinks at the Silver Dollar.

With all the excitement going on, Willie failed to notice a tall lanky man dressed in a blue officer's coat walk inside the gaming house and stroll to the bar. The man carried two shiny revolvers and spoke with an accent that belonged along the Missouri, most likely at Kansas City.

Someone at the bar heard him called Johnson.

CHAPTER 20

Ψ

Colonel Courtney brought two other gentlemen from the railroad to play that evening. By the look of them, both were wealthy and used to spending freely. Bottles of wine were set out beside the gaming table, and the card playing began in earnest.

Willie was struck by the thought that his earlier success might simply have been a prelude to this game. Such men as the Colonel and his companions would hardly play for dollar stakes.

The high stakes didn't seem to improve the play of the colonel, though, and his companions were little better. Willie found they had come to play in order to sample the kind of man Texas cattle might bring to Abilene.

The first player, a fat giant named Baldwin, held interest in three major lines. The other, a smaller man with roaming eyes, called himself Gaines. Gaines was a shrewd poker player, but Baldwin was all noise. Willie assumed from the worn corners of Gaines's sleeves and collar that there was need to be cautious in a game of chance. A poor man hardly had money to throw to the wind.

As they played, the colonel offered Willie glass after glass of the wine. Willie wasn't a heavy drinking man, and he found it easier to keep a full glass at his side than to drink and have more offered.

Willie's luck held him even through the game, while the clever Mr. Gaines won heavily. As the play continued, Willie thought he caught a sparkle of friendship in the small man's eye.

"Are you married, young man?" Gains asked.

"I hope to be soon," Willie said.

"Girl back home? Off a farm, no doubt."

"My sister," Travis said, passing a small photograph of Ellen to the gentlemen.

"Lovely," Gaines said, throwing in his hand. "Have you thought of settling up here someplace? The railroad offers many fine opportunities for a man with courage."

"I have a home, sir," Willie said. "There are those who died so it could be mine."

"I see," Gaines said. "I understand and commend you on your loyalty."

Willie won that hand, overpowering three of the colonel's sevens with three tens. Courtney downed another glass of wine, and Gaines laughed.

"You seem to have got under the colonel's skin," Gaines whispered to Willie when the colonel walked to the bar. "He fancies himself quite a player at cards."

"He bets too much on his own cards," Willie said. "He never allows for the other man having a hand."

"A bad habit when facing a Texas full house," Gaines said. "But he wins enough from others to lose to you and me. It's about all that keeps me going. I've no head for business at all."

Willie smiled. He wouldn't do business with the small man anymore than he'd invite a rattlesnake to share his bed.

The colonel returned then, and the game went on. When it dragged into its third hour, Willie felt something touch his shoulder. A shadow fell over the table, and he became aware of a man standing behind him.

"If you're not party to this game, sir, I'd rather you stand clear of the table," Colonel Courtney said.

"It makes me nervous to have someone looking over my cards," Willie said, putting down his hand and turning to face the man.

"I don't care if it makes you cry like a baby, Texas," the man answered.

A hush fell over the room, and Gaines shook as he prepared to start the betting.

"I'll open," Colonel Courtney said.

"Not until this man leaves, Colonel," Willie said, shoving the money away from the center of the table.

"Sir, I must insist," Gaines said, his face begging the tall man to back away from the table.

"You got no call to insist nothin'," the man behind Willie said. "There ain't no law about watching a card game."

"We can finish the game in my hotel room," Willie said, standing up.

"Finish it here!" the man said, slamming Willie back into the chair.

It took only a minute for Willie to respond. Gritting his teeth so as not to show how painful the shoulder was, Willie let fly with a right hand that knocked the intruder to the floor of the saloon.

"You'll pay for that, Texas," the man said, opening his coat so that the shiny revolver on each hip could be seen. "Make your play."

"Gentlemen, please!" Gaines said.

Willie motioned everyone out of the way, though. The occupants of the room filed out the swinging doors to the street or hid behind the bar. Only Travis Cobb and a few of the ranch hands stayed in the room, cautiously keeping an eye out for any friends of the stranger who might get into the act.

"I've killed men before," Willie said, swallowing his uneasiness. "More than five this summer."

"Not eye to eye, I expect," the other man said. "I've cut down close to twenty in my time."

Willie looked into the man's cold gray eyes. A gunfighter for sure, a man to whom killing was a way of life. But death was Willie's shadow, wasn't it? And his own eyes turned cold and cruel as well.

"You bring this on yourself," Willie said. "What name do you want put on your tombstone?"

"Hah," the man said, smiling brightly. "You've got a boldness to you, that's for sure. You fight like you play cards. Well, tell the devil it was Frank Johnson that sent you his way."

"Frank Johnson," some of the men behind them mumbled in a way that told Willie the man was not without a reputation in the part of the country.

"Anytime you're ready, Johnson," Willie said, readying his hand.

The stranger wet his lips in anticipation of the duel. Willie saw that the man enjoyed the killing, the excitement. Such a man would die sooner or later. And Willie had more to do with his life.

The cold determination, the anger that had brought him through a war, through Comanche raids and cattle drives came back to him. His eyes flashed that chilling anger across to Johnson, and the killer's smile fell away.

It was Johnson's hand that moved first, taking the twin revolvers from their holsters even as Willie drew his Colt. One of Johnson's shots struck the great mirror behind the bar. The other blasted through the floorboards at his feet. The single shot fired from Willie's level pistol blew a small round hole in Johnson's chest just below the left pocket of his jacket.

People moved all at once, some to congratulate Willie, others to tend the mortally wounded Johnson. Willie leaned against Travis a moment, then stared at Johnson.

"Who?" the fallen gunman asked. "Who are you?"

"Does it matter?" Willie asked.

"It matters!" the man shouted, silencing the spectators with the fury of his speech.

"You've been killed, man," Colonel Courtney said. "Do you wish to see our reverend?"

"No preachers," Johnson said, blood leaking from his mouth as he spoke. "Who are you?"

Willie motioned the others away and knelt beside the dying man.

"Willie Delamer," he whispered.

"What?" the man asked, his fingers trembling as he grabbed Willie's shirt. "Delamer?"

"That's right," Willie said, prying the man's fingers off his shirt.

There was a stirring behind them, and the people moved aside to allow Sam Delamer to reach his brother.

"Are you hurt, Willie?" Sam asked. "I heard shots."

"I'm fine," Willie said, surprised at his brother's quick arrival.

"Delamer," Johnson mumbled, the blood covering his lips as his lungs collapsed. "Why?"

Willie started to say something, but he saw in the man's eyes that the question hadn't been directed toward him. Johnson reached his hand out to Sam, but the older of the Delamers pulled back. Willie watched his brother's face grow pale with terror.

"Sam?" Willie said, trembling from head to toe.

"The man's delirious," Sam said, standing up. "If you're all right I'm going back to my work."

Willie turned back to Johnson and stared as the man drew three crisp hundred dollar bills from his pocket. Clutching them against his bloody chest, Johnson gasped for air.

"Half," the gunman mumbled, collapsing against Willie's side. "Half in advance."

Then the man's eyes froze, and the breathing ceased. Willie laid the man's head on the floor and stepped away, wiping blood from his hands as he might once have removed dirt at the river bank.

"Let's have some music!" someone called out, and the

151

piano player hammered out a merry tune, only a little off-key.

"Drinks on the house!" the saloon owner yelled, and the crowd around Johnson abandoned him in favor of the bar.

"Who suggested this game?" Willie asked, turning to Colonel Courtney. "My brother?"

"Oh, no," Gaines said, shaking his head. "Actually it was your brother who asked about you."

"And you told him I'd be playing cards this evening?"

"Yes, we . . . no, it was the colonel who did."

"Yes," Colonel Courtney said. "I believe it was me. Your brother's interest seemed rather strange as a matter of fact. Up to that point I don't remember him saying a word about you."

"I trust you'll excuse me from the game," Willie said.

"Yes, of course," Gaines said. "We will expect you to give us another chance at that Texas luck of yours."

"I don't think that's likely," Willie said. "I'll be going home soon."

"And your winnings, sir?" Gaines asked.

Willie glanced across the gaming table at Travis Cobb.

"Pick them up for me, will you, Trav?" Willie asked. "I've got something to do."

"Willie, you're not planning to do something stupid, are you?" Travis asked, pulling Willie away from the door. "You'd best sit down and have a drink."

"I don't need one," Willie said, knocking a glass of whiskey from the hand of a man who offered it.

"You need something," Travis said.

"All I need is about ten minutes of my dear brother's time," Willie said, his eyes full of rage.

"You're not going over there like this," Travis said. "You'll do something you'll be sorry for later. I've seen that look before, Willie. Somebody usually dies when you get like this."

"And what should I do, lie around like a dog and wait for somebody else to come after me, huh, Trav? You heard that man. Three hundred in advance. Half! I'm worth six

152

hundred dollars. And who do you suppose put up that money?"

"Calm down," Travis said, motioning for two men to help hold Willie back. "We all heard it. We'll tell the sheriff."

"Sheriff? In a town like this? You talk to the sheriff," Willie said. "I'm going."

Travis fought to hold him back. Then someone grabbed Travis.

"Let him go," Les Cobb said to his brother. "It's time Sam Delamer had what was coming to him."

The others grumbled their agreement, and Willie escaped.

"Willie, come back!" Travis called out. "He's your brother!"

But Willie had no ears for anything that was said. He was feeling mean, ready to strike out at something or someone. And that someone was named Sam Delamer.

CHAPTER 21

Ψ

Willie charged past the desk clerk and bulled his way up the stairs to Sam's room. The door was slightly ajar, and Willie paused to listen. Hearing nothing, he kicked the door open and drew his pistol. But when he entered the room, he found Sam sitting behind a table, studying the ledgers.

"I thought it might be you, Willie," Sam said. "No one else around here kicks doors open."

"I want to talk to you!" Willie shouted.

"Then talk," Sam said, closing the book. "But hurry. I plan to eat dinner soon."

Willie looked at his brother through eyes filled with rage. He could hardly control his anger, and it was with difficulty that he replaced the revolver in its holster.

"I came up here to ask you why you did it," Willie said. "I don't quite understand."

"Did what?" Sam asked.

"You know what!" Willie screamed. "You and every man in that saloon heard him call out your name. He asked you, and now I am. Why?"

"You're confused, Willie," Sam said, his hands trembling slightly. "He called your name."

"No, he was looking right at you, Sam. And everyone in that room knew it. He sure wasn't asking me why I shot him. Any fool knew that. No, he wanted to know why Sam Delamer would pay six hundred dollars to have his brother killed."

"It had to have been someone else using my name," Sam said.

"Oh?" Willie asked. "Then just how did you know when to come into the saloon? How'd he know it was me? You set the whole thing up. You couldn't hear a gunshot from up here, and you sure wouldn't come running over there to see if it was me that got shot. You asked Colonel Courtney if we would be playing cards. Then you saw to it your friend broke up the game. You had it all figured."

"Before walking into that saloon, I never in all my life saw Johnson."

"Then how'd you know his name?" Willie asked. "He only said it once, and that was before the gunplay. You might not have seen him, but you paid him to do it. Six hundred dollars! Is that all my life's worth?"

"You're excited," Sam said, standing up. "You'd best calm down."

"I'll calm down when I'm finished!" Willie shouted angrily. "There are some things to clear up. First, I want an agreement turning over control of the ranch to me."

"I'm through signing agreements," Sam said, looking away from his brother.

"You'll sign this one," Willie said, grabbing Sam's arm and forcing him to turn around. "You'll sign this one, or I'll go to the sheriff."

"You don't have any hard evidence," Sam said. "No court would convict me on your suspicions."

"Maybe not, but I wouldn't be so sure. And the newspapers might like the story. How would Helen and her New Orleans family like to read about their Sam, the man who hired a gunman to shoot his brother?"

"You'd never do that," Sam said. "The blessed family name means more to you than it means to me."

Willie frowned. Sam was right about that. He wouldn't see mud splashed on the Delamer name if it was avoidable.

"When did you decide to have it done, Sam? When we left? Or did it come to you lately?"

"In Wichita, as a matter of fact," Sam said.

"Not in Wichita," Willie said. "I'd just saved your life."

"That was your mistake, not mine," Sam said. "If it had been the other way around, you would have been buried by that stampede. No, I thought about it after the Kiowa raid. I knew then that the hands would stand by you if it ever came to a showdown. The only way for the ranch to grow was for you to die."

"You owe your life to me, Sam," Willie said. "And the herd. I got us here, not you. I found the guide, got the men. You'd never have made it on your own."

"Sure enough, Willie. Let's see."

Sam opened a small black box and counted out a hundred dollars. He handed the money over and smiled.

"Top wages for a foreman, Willie," Sam said. "And ten more to get you on your way. You're fired!"

"I didn't sign on as any foreman, Sam! I took to the trail as a full partner. I worked double to cover James's share. The profits are going to be split three ways."

"The profits go to the ranch, to pay taxes and expand. Colonel Courtney says there'll be a railroad cutting through Texas bound for California."

"So now you're going to buy a railroad. Sam, I have a say in all this. Papa left a will, and . . ."

"Not that again," Sam said. "Do you really want to know what Papa said in that will? He wanted James to finish his schooling and for you to have a job on the ranch as long as you needed it. He figured you'd want to head farther west and pioneer."

"You're lying," Willie said, grinding his teeth.

"No, and it's what would be best. Take Ellen Cobb off

to Colorado. Mary's done well out there. I'll even give you a thousand dollars to get you started."

"Don't do me any favors," Willie said.

"It's cheaper than hiring another Johnson. And I will, little brother. I'll keep hiring them until I find one who does a proper job of it."

"In the back, no doubt," Willie said. "It's your style."

"Whatever gets the job done," Sam said.

"You'd do it without feeling a thing, wouldn't you?" Willie asked. "How long have you hated me, Sam?"

"Since the day you were born," Sam said, the bitterness flowing across his face. "Papa gave you his name, and you were always the special one. I did what he asked, went to school, learned how to manage the business. But it was always Willie this, Willie that. You could do no wrong.

"Mama was almost as bad. She'd clean you up when you scraped your legs or got your arm sliced by the Comanches. When it was over, she'd cry over you instead of thrashing your hide. And when you should have gone away to school, you took off buffalo hunting with the Indians. Mama and Papa cried over you and gave in.

"You took them away from me, Willie," Sam said. "They never loved me like they did you. I could understand it with James. He was so much smaller, but you weren't much younger than I was. Five years isn't so much."

"If that's true, then it wasn't my doing," Willie said. "I always looked up to you, Sam. You never did the things papa loved. Hunting, fishing . . . that's what drew us together. He could've ridden all day, and you didn't take to horses. You were never interested in the old ways. If Papa loved me better, it was because I was him. I always knew what he was thinking and feeling. I don't know how, but that's the way it was."

"You were even there when he died," Sam said.

"That was your choice, too. He wanted you to go with him, remember? He asked you. You stayed with Helen."

"She was due to have our child," Sam said.

"But it was your choice," Willie said. "You didn't stay

once you left. You came back after Elkhorn Tavern with your tail between your legs."

"I did my duty there," Sam said.

"You sat on your horse and watched the men die," Willie said. "I heard all about it. Your company rode through Corinth when I was getting my health back."

"I was never cut out to be a soldier," Sam said.

"No, Sam, you were cut out for ledgers and telegraphs. But a ranch doesn't get run that way. Sometimes you have to ride the hills yourself, let the men know you're with them. They'll work for a ledger book and ten dollars a month, but they won't die for it. They would've died for Bill Delamer."

"And you?"

"And me, if I asked them," Willie said. "And me for them. They know that, Sam. The thing you still don't understand is that I would've died for you, too."

Willie's eyes were swollen with emotion. The rage had given way to something else, a deep kind of sadness that seemed to overwhelm everything else.

"Get out of here, Willie!" Sam screamed. "Find yourself another world to live in. All the Trident Ranch can bring you is a grave on that little knoll."

"I can't ride away from that place anymore than I can cut my head off. I belong to that land. I'm tied to it. It's part of me, my heart and soul. I can breathe and eat and sleep somewhere else, but I can't live away from those cliffs, from the river."

"There's no place for you there," Sam said. "If you try to come back, somebody will put a bullet between your shoulders."

"No!" Willie yelled.

"Oh, yes. And even if I took you back there as a partner it wouldn't last. Sooner or later one of us has to be top dog. There would be more bloodshed. I won't have that! I have sons and a daughter. I mean to build the ranch for them."

"And James?"

"He'll have his law office," Sam said. "He can handle

the legal affairs and share in the profits. I like James. Maybe he doesn't look to me with the kind of feeling he has for you, but I've been a father to him for four years."

"You've got it all figured out, don't you?" Willie asked.

"I have for a long time," Sam said. "We don't want you back, Willie. There's no room for you to grow. You're not Bill Delamer, you're someone else. Find out who and come visit. But don't plan to stay too long."

"The time will come when you'll need me, Sam," Willie said. "Someone or something comes along that can't be cheated or lied away, and you'll have need of a strong man like Papa to meet it head on. You don't have what it takes inside you, Sam."

"And you do?" Sam asked. "No, Willie, you're the weak one! A strong man takes what he wants. Like me. Like Papa. No, if you were strong you'd pull out that pistol and shoot me dead. Then it would all be yours."

"You don't understand much about me," Willie said. "Or about being strong. It'd be easy to kill you."

Willie pulled out his gun and cocked the trigger. He then swung the pistol around so that Sam's forehead filled the sights.

"Easy," Willie said, smiling wickedly. "But I'm strong enough to walk away, Sam, even though leaving for me is like dying. You see, I value who I am. I'm like the old one. He left France rather than toss away that old sword the king gave him. I'm who I am."

"Yes, you are that," Sam said. "I almost feel sorry for you, Willie. But you could never rule the Trident. Only a really strong man can hold the reins of such a ranch."

"You may find a pair of spurs big enough to grind out the spirit of that place, Sam, but you'll never be able to touch its soul. You'll never hold the soil in your hands and know it belongs to you. Not in those hands of yours! They can only spoil anything they touch, and everyone!"

"You're a fool, Willie Delamer," Sam said, laughing.

Willie felt his hand tremble as he touched the trigger of

the Colt revolver. At the last minute he moved the gun to one side and blew a hole in the wall beside Sam's head.

"God, you could have hit me!" Sam screamed.

"You might remember just how close you came to getting what you deserve, Sam. And maybe when you lie in bed some winter's night, you'll remember I'm still out there somewhere, thinking about what you did."

There was a noise in the hall outside then, and Travis Cobb charged into the room.

"For God's sake put that pistol down, Willie," Travis said. "The clerk's gone for the sheriff."

"Let Sam tell him all about Mr. Johnson," Willie said. "I seem to smell something rotten in here."

Willie holstered his gun and turned away from his brother.

"You want the money?" Sam called to him.

"I'd burn it first," Willie said.

After pausing long enough to remove his gear from the room next door, Willie followed Travis downstairs and the two old friends walked together through the door into the dying light of day.

"I thought you killed him," Travis said.

"Disappointed?" Willie asked.

"Some," Travis said. "It would've made it simpler for a lot of us."

"I came close to doing it, Trav," Willie said. "Closer than I would've thought possible. But he's my brother."

As they wound their way down the street toward the stable, Willie turned and glanced back at the hotel. He saw Sam's face staring at him from the window, hatred in his eyes. Willie glared up at his brother, clashing his cold eyes in such a way that the air seemed to grow cold. When Willie finally turned and continued toward the stable, a strange feeling came over him. Somehow he knew that was the last time he'd ever see Sam in the world of the living.

CHAPTER 22

Ψ

Willie slept that night in the stable. His dreams were filled over and over again by the picture of Sam's head in his pistol sights. More than once that head was blown apart by the force of a .45 caliber bullet.

When Willie finally woke the next morning, he was afraid for the first time in memory. When facing the Comanches or the cattle rustlers, with death so close he could smell it, he'd never been so scared. He knew it was because he'd always known his enemy before. Now he was frightened. And it was that something inside him which pulled the trigger in his dreams that brought the fear.

It didn't take long to pack his things. The old war chest had made the long trek north in the cook's wagon. Willie now took it to the railroad freight office and paid to have it shipped west, as far as was possible.

Willie went to the bank then and withdrew the money he'd put on deposit there. Barton peeled off the bills with the greatest of reluctance, telling Willie all the while about a high stakes game Gaines had organized in Baldwin's fancy railway car for that evening.

"I'll be on my way before then," Willie said. "I never found a town too comfortable for long."

When all was made ready, Willie walked to the Silver Dollar and found Travis. His old friend was involved in a small game of stud with Les and two farmers. Travis made his apologies and accompanied Willie to the stable.

"I'm leaving," Willie said simply. "I need a favor or two from you, though."

"Anything I got's yours," Travis said.

"I know that," Willie said. "But it's not things I need from you."

"Then it's got to do with Ellen," Travis said. "She'll go to Colorado or anywhere with you. You know that."

"I know," Willie said.

"And here," Travis said, pulling out a roll of bills and placing them in Willie's hands. "Your poker winnings are enough of a stake for ten men."

"I know that, too," Willie said. "But I can't take her where I'm going. I'm not sure where it'll be for one thing. The other is I'm not sure what I'll be when I get there.

"I never belonged anywhere but walking those cliffs beside the Brazos. I put my heart in the ground there a long time ago. I don't figure I'll find it in some cornfield in Colorado. It's like Five Forks all over again, except this time there's no place to run to."

"There's room on our place for another man," Travis said.

"What kind of a future could I offer anybody there? Sam can't have me in the valley. Sooner or later some Johnson would come for me."

"If you went back now, the hands would rally to you. To a man, Willie. Sam'd find he wasn't welcome."

"If it was just Sam, that'd be fine. But he's got kids. I won't look into my own nephews' eyes and see the kind of hate I've got for Sam. No, I can't ever go back to the valley."

"And Ellen?"

"She's not so old as to be having a hard time finding a man, Trav," Willie said. "She hasn't known many."

"She'll come after you," Travis said.

"No, not after you explain it to her," Willie said.

"Explain what?" Travis asked. "I don't understand a bit of this."

"You don't have to," Willie said, sighing. "Just say what I tell you. Say there was this accident. Railroad car ran me down just this side of Abilene. Say I spoke her name as I was dying. And give her the money."

Willie handed Travis back the poker winnings and tried to smile.

"I can't take this," Travis said.

"It's for a house a fine one," Willie said. "You buy it for Ellen. Don't say how you came by the money. Maybe later when she's got her kids all grown, you can tell her the rest. But for now, just say that I'm dead."

"I'd argue with you, Willie, but it's the best thing for Ellen. I knew that a long time ago. But I worry about you. Where'll you go? What are you going to do?"

"There's always work for a man that knows horses," Willie said. "I can work hard. Maybe getting away from the ranch, away from Papa's memories and everybody who knew me in the war might get me sorted out some. I might even get out to Mary's place in Colorado."

"You don't believe that anymore than I do," Travis said.

"If you ever get to needing me, you write to James. I'll keep in touch with him."

"You'd best take this," Travis said, handing Willie the old watch with Ellen's cameo portrait on the inside.

"No, you keep it, Trav," Willie said. "I don't think I could ride away with something to remind me of her. I don't mind so much the rest of it, leaving the ranch and James and all. But I won't find anyone like Ellen where I'll be going."

"We had some fine times, Willie. Riding the Shenandoah and chasing Yanks. Running through the river and hooking catfish."

163

"You watch yourself, Trav," Willie said, swallowing his sadness. "Remember me sometimes to your kids."

"Likely we'll have a lot of boys named Willie in our family," Travis said, trying to smile.

"If you do, take 'em up to the cliffs sometimes. Tell 'em about the ancient ones and the Comanches. Explain about Red Wolf's grave, and how Willie Delamer put him there."

"I will," Travis said.

The two old friends clasped hands, gripping each other's wrists so that one might have thought the flesh had grown together. Then they drew apart, and Willie mounted old Thunder.

"Look out for yourself, Willie," Travis called to him.

"You, too," Willie said, pausing long enough to look a final time at Travis Cobb. "And look in on Ellen."

"You know I will," Travis said, waving farewell.

Willie turned Thunder and headed out the main street. The rising sun was over his left shoulder, and he stared ahead at the mysterious western horizon. The unknown lurked there, waiting for him.

As he cleared the outskirts of Abilene, he gave a final thought to Ellen. Passing between the river and the shiny new rails of the colonel's railroad, he could almost sense the warmth of her hand on his shoulder. He stopped a moment and stared at the river.

He'd always thought it strange that rivers should look so much alike. The water of the Kansas was just as he remembered the Brazos. It was the same thought that had come to his mind the first time he'd viewed the Tennessee and the Shenandoah and the James. Rivers were much the same.

The wind whined through the branches of a nearby cottonwood, singing a ghostly chant that might have been heard in a village where Comanches once camped. Cattle would run there that autumn. Willie urged Thunder on, sighing as the song faded away behind him.

Willie stared once more at the river beside him. He watched the waters tear at the bank, reshaping the basin as the moments went by. Everything changes, he thought to himself. He wished for a second that some great hand would reach down from the clouds and hold off the onslaught of time. It was no more than an idle wish, though, and there was no great disappointment inside him when it didn't come to pass. He'd grown accustomed to the hardness of reality.

Suddenly he heard a voice calling to him out of the past. It was a deep solemn kind of an echo, ringing through the rainy evening of that first day at Shiloh. The promise. It had been forgotten.

"Papa, I tried," Willie whispered. "But so much changed. I did. Sam did. The world did. I'm sorry, but it couldn't be."

Willie shivered with a chill brought by a strange trickle of moisture that worked its way down his cheeks. He rubbed his eyes with his shirt-sleeve, and the wind brushed away what was left of the moisture. There would be no more tears, he told himself.

He straightened his shoulders and spit to one side. The sadness flowed out of him into the barren Kansas hillside. He urged Thunder forward at a trot. There were miles to be covered, rivers to ford, mountains to climb. But he knew that no matter how clear and beautiful, wide or tall, none of them would ever be called home.

ABOUT THE AUTHOR

G. Clifton Wisler comes by his interest in the West naturally. Born in Oklahoma and raised in Texas, he discovered early on a fascination for the history of the region. His first novel, MY BROTHER, THE WIND, received a nomination for the American Book Award in 1980. Among the thirteen others that have followed are THUNDER ON THE TENNESSEE, winner of the Western Writers of America Spur Award for Best Western Juvenile Novel of 1983; WINTER OF THE WOLF, a Spur finalist in 1982; and Delamer Westerns STARR'S SHOWDOWN and THE TRIDENT BRAND. After twelve years teaching in the Texas public schools, Wisler now devotes his time to writing and speaking to school groups. He lives in Garland, Texas, where he is active in Boy Scouts.

FAWCETT ROUNDS UP THE Best of the West